Additional Praise for

Kudos

"Coolly detached, narcotically gorgeous . . . Like all great art, this novel consistently eludes us in leaps of grace and daring . . . [*Outline*, *Transit*, and *Kudos*] are texts, finally, to read and revisit, lean, oracular, irreducible."
—*Los Angeles Times*

"Cusk has glimpsed the central truth of modern life . . . She moves through it as a blasted center full only of instinct and superhuman hearing and hackles."
—Patricia Lockwood, *London Review of Books*

"This important trilogy, then, through its eloquent polyphony of voices and opinions, arrives at an idea of feminist art in opposition to the confessional mode that has long been in ascendance. Ms. Cusk's tools are ambivalence and elusiveness—or, to rearrange James Joyce's terms of independence: exile, cunning, and silence."
—Sam Sacks, *The Wall Street Journal*

"The effect is of watching an oracle divine fearsome and inscrutable truths from on high, then render them into stories fit for mortals . . . Mesmerizing."
—Jordan Larson, *New York* magazine's *The Cut*

ABOUT THE AUTHOR

RACHEL CUSK is the author of the *Outline* trilogy; the memoirs *A Life's Work, The Last Supper,* and *Aftermath*; and several other novels. She is the recipient of a Guggenheim Fellowship. She lives in Norfolk, England.

ALSO BY RACHEL CUSK

FICTION

NONFICTION

KUDOS

RACHEL CUSK

PICADOR

FARRAR, STRAUS AND GIROUX

New York

KUDOS. Copyright © 2018 by Rachel Cusk. All rights reserved. Printed in the United States of America. For information, address Picador, 175 Fifth Avenue, New York, N.Y. 10010.

picadorusa.com • instagram.com/picador
twitter.com/picadorusa • facebook.com/picadorusa

Picador® is a U.S. registered trademark and is used by Macmillan Publishing Group, LLC, under license from Pan Books Limited.

For book club information, please visit facebook.com/picadorbookclub or email marketing@picadorusa.com.

Grateful acknowledgment is made for permission to reprint an excerpt from "She Got Up and Went Away," from *The Collected Poems & Drawings of Steve Smith*, ed. Will May, © Estate of James MacGibbon and reprinted by permission of Faber and Faber Limited.

The Library of Congress has cataloged the Farrar, Straus and Giroux edition as follows:

Names: Cusk, Rachel, 1967– author.
Title: Kudos / Rachel Cusk.
Description: First American edition. | New York : Farrar, Straus and Giroux, 2018.
Identifiers: LCCN 2018002527 | ISBN 9780374279868 (hardcover)
Subjects: LCSH Authors—Fiction. | Europe—Fiction.
Classification: LCC PR6053.U825 K83 2018 | DDC 823'.914—dc23
LC record available at https://lccn.loc.gov/2018002527

Picador Paperback ISBN 978-1-250-20739-5

Our books may be purchased in bulk for promotional, educational, or business use. Please contact your local bookseller or the Macmillan Corporate and Premium Sales Department at 1-800-221-7945, extension 5442, or by email at MacmillanSpecialMarkets@macmillan.com.

Originally published in Great Britain by Faber and Faber Limited

First published in the United States by Farrar, Straus and Giroux

First Picador Edition: April 2019

10 9 8 7 6 5 4 3 2 1

She got up and went away
Should she not have? Not have what?
Got up and gone away.

Yes, I think she should have
Because it was getting darker.

Getting what? Darker. Well,
There was still some
Day left when she went away, well,
Enough to see the way.
And it was the last time she would have
   been able . . .
Able? . . . to get up and go away.
It was the last time the very last time for
After that she could not
Have got up and gone away any more.

　　　'She Got Up and Went Away', Stevie Smith

The man next to me on the plane was so tall he couldn't fit in his seat. His elbows jutted out over the armrests and his knees were jammed against the seat in front, so that the person in it glanced around in irritation every time he moved. The man twisted, trying to cross and uncross his legs, and inadvertently kicked the person to his right.

'Sorry,' he said.

He sat motionless for a few minutes, breathing deeply through his nostrils with his hands clenched in his lap, but before long he became restless and tried to move his legs again so that the whole bank of seats in front of him was jolted back and forth. Finally I asked him if he wanted to change seats, since mine was on the aisle, and he accepted with alacrity, as if I had offered him a business opportunity.

'Usually I travel in executive class,' he explained, while we got up and changed places. 'There's a lot more legroom.'

He stretched out into the aisle and his head fell against the back of the seat in relief.

'Thank you very much,' he said.

The plane began to move slowly out over the tarmac. My neighbour gave a contented sigh and appeared almost instantly to fall asleep. An air hostess came up the aisle and stopped at his legs.

'Sir?' she said. 'Sir?'

He jerked awake and folded himself awkwardly back into the narrow space in front so that she could pass. The plane paused for a few minutes and then lurched forward and then paused again. Through the window a queue of planes could be seen ahead, waiting their turn. The man's head began to nod and soon his legs were splayed once more across the aisle. The air hostess returned.

'Sir?' she said. 'We need to keep the aisle clear for take-off.'

He sat up.

'Sorry,' he said.

She moved away and gradually his head began to nod again. Outside a haze stood over the flat grey landscape so that it seemed to merge with the overcast sky in horizontal bands of such subtle variation that it almost resembled the sea. In the seats in front a woman and a man were talking. It's so sad, the woman said, and the man grunted in reply. It's just really sad, she repeated. There was a pounding of footsteps up the carpeted aisle and the air hostess reappeared. She put her hand on my neighbour's shoulder and shook it.

'I'm afraid I'm going to have to ask you to keep your legs out of the way,' she said.

'I'm sorry,' the man said. 'I can't seem to stay awake.'

'I'm going to have to ask that you do,' she said.

'I didn't actually get to bed last night,' he said.

'I'm afraid that's not my problem,' she said. 'You're putting other passengers at risk by obstructing the aisle.'

He rubbed his face and rearranged himself in his chair. He took out his phone and checked it and put it back in his pocket. She waited, watching him. Finally, as though satisfied that he had genuinely obeyed her, she went away. He shook his head and made a gesture of incomprehension, as though to an unseen audience. He was somewhere in his forties, with a face that was both handsome and unexceptional, and his tall frame was clad with the clean, well-pressed neutrality of a businessman's weekend attire. He wore a heavy silver watch on his wrist and new-looking leather shoes on his feet; he exuded an air of anonymous and slightly provisional manliness, like a soldier in uniform. By now the plane had made its halting progress up the queue and was slowly turning in a wide arc towards the runway. The haze had turned to rain and droplets ran down the window pane. The man looked out with an exhausted stare at the gleaming tarmac. The clamour of the engines was rising around us and the plane finally surged forward, then rose tipping and rattling through layers of thick wadded cloud. For a while the dull green network of fields beneath us with its block-like houses and huddled groups of trees returned to sight through sporadic rents in the grey before it closed over them. The man emitted another deep sigh and in a few minutes had gone back to sleep, his head lolling forward over his chest. The cabin lights flickered on and the sounds of activity began. Before long the air hostess was at our row, where the sleeping man had once more stretched his legs out into the aisle.

'Sir?' she said. 'Excuse me? Sir?'

He lifted his head and looked around himself, bewildered. When he saw the air hostess standing there with her trolley he slowly and effortfully withdrew his legs so that she could pass. She watched with pursed lips, her eyebrows arched.

'Thank you,' she said, with barely concealed sarcasm.

'It's not my fault,' he said to her.

Her painted eyes fell on him momentarily. Their expression was cold.

'I'm just trying to do my job,' she said.

'I realise that,' he said. 'But it's not my fault that the seats are too close together.'

There was a pause in which the two of them looked at one another.

'You'll have to take that up with the airline,' she said.

'I'm taking it up with you,' he said.

She folded her arms and lifted her chin.

'Most of the time I travel business,' he said, 'so it isn't usually a problem.'

'We don't offer business class on this flight,' she said. 'But there are plenty of other carriers who do.'

'So your suggestion is that I fly with someone else,' he said.

'That's right,' she said.

'Brilliant,' he said. 'Thank you very much.'

He gave a sour bark of laughter at her departing back. For a while he continued to smile self-consciously, like someone who has mistakenly wandered out onstage, and then, apparently to disguise his feelings of exposure, he turned to me and asked the reason for my trip to Europe.

I said I was a writer and was on my way to speak at a literary festival.

Immediately his face assumed an expression of polite interest.

'My wife's a big reader,' he said. 'She belongs to one of those book clubs.'

A silence fell.

'What kind of thing do you write?' he said, after a while.

I said it was hard to explain and he nodded his head. He drummed his fingers on his thighs and tapped a disjointed rhythm with his shoes on the carpeted floor. He shook his head from side to side and rubbed his fingers vigorously over his scalp.

'If I don't talk,' he said finally, 'I'll just go to sleep again.'

He said it pragmatically, as though he was used to solving problems at the expense of personal feeling, but when I turned to look at him I was surprised to see a pleading expression on his face. His eyes were red-rimmed with yellow whites and his neatly cut hair stood on end where he had rubbed it.

'Apparently they lower the oxygen levels in the cabin before take-off to make people sleepy,' he said, 'so they shouldn't really complain when it works. I have a friend who flies these things,' he added. 'He was the one who told me that.'

The strange thing about this friend, the man went on, was that despite his profession he was a fanatical environmentalist. He drove a tiny electric car and ran his household entirely on solar panels and windmills.

'When he comes to our place for dinner,' he said, 'you'll find him out by the recycling bins while everyone else is four sheets to the wind, sorting the food packaging and the empties. His idea of a holiday,' he said, 'is carrying all his own gear up a Welsh mountainside and sitting in a tent in the rain for two weeks talking to the sheep.'

Yet this same man regularly donned a uniform and climbed into the cockpit of a fifty-ton smoke-spewing machine and flew a cabin-load of drunken holiday-makers to the Canary Islands. It was hard to think of a worse route to fly, yet his friend had flown it for years. He worked for a budget airline that practised the most brutal economies, and apparently the passengers behaved like zoo animals. He took them out white and he brought them back orange, and despite earning less than anyone else in their circle of friends, he gave half his income to charity.

'The thing is,' he said perplexedly, 'he's just a really nice guy. I've known him for years, and it's almost like the worse things are, the nicer he becomes. He told me once,' he said, 'that in the cockpit they have a screen where they can watch what's going on in the cabin. He said that at first he couldn't stand looking at it because it was so depressing seeing the way these people conducted themselves. But after a while he started to become sort of obsessed with it. He's watched hundreds of hours of it. It's a bit like meditation, he says. Even so,' he said, 'I wouldn't be able to stand working in that world. The first thing I did when I retired was cut up my frequent flyer's card. I swore I'd never get on one of these things again.'

I said he seemed very young to be retired.

'I kept a spreadsheet on my desktop called "Freedom",' he said, with a sideways grin. 'It was basically just columns of figures that had to add up to a certain number, and when they did I could leave.'

He had been the director of a global management company, he said, a job that involved being constantly away from home. For example, it wasn't unusual for him to visit Asia, North America and Australia all in the space of two weeks. He had once flown to South Africa for a meeting and flown back again as soon as the meeting was over. Several times, he and his wife had worked out where the halfway point was between their two locations and then met there for a holiday. Once, when the company's Australasian branch had gone into meltdown and he'd had to stay over there to sort it out, he hadn't seen his children for three months. He'd started work at eighteen and now he was forty-six, and he hoped he would have enough time to live the whole of his working life in reverse. He had a house in the Cotswolds he'd barely set foot in and a whole garage full of bikes and skis and sporting equipment he'd never had time to use; he had friends and family he'd spent the past two decades mostly saying hello and goodbye to, since he was usually either going away and had to prepare and go to bed early, or coming back exhausted. He had read somewhere about a medieval method of punishment that involved incarcerating the prisoner in a space specially designed to prevent him from being able to fully extend his limbs in any direction, and though just thinking about it made him break out in a sweat, it pretty much summed up the way he had lived.

I asked him whether his release from that prison had lived up to the title of his spreadsheet.

'It's funny you should say that,' he said. 'Since I left work I find that I'm constantly getting into arguments with people. My family complain that now I'm at home all the time, I'm trying to control them. They haven't actually said,' he added, 'that they wish we could go back to how things were. But I know they're thinking it.'

He couldn't believe, for example, how late they slept in the morning. All those years that he'd left the house before dawn, the thought of their slumbering forms in the darkness had often made him feel purposeful and protective. If he'd realised how idle they were he might not have seen it the same way. Sometimes he had to wait until lunchtime for them to get up: he had started going into their rooms and opening the curtains, as his father used to do every morning when he was growing up, and was astonished by the hostility this action elicited. He had tried to schedule their mealtimes – they all, he had discovered, ate different foods at different times of day – and to institute an exercise routine, and was trying hard to believe that the full-scale revolt these measures provoked was proof of their necessity.

'I spend a lot of time talking to the cleaner,' he said. 'She turns up at eight. She says she's been dealing with these issues for years.'

He recounted all this with an abashed and easy confidentiality that made it clear he spoke for the purposes of entertainment rather than to arouse consternation. A deprecating smile played around his mouth, showing an even row of strong white teeth. He had grown more animated while he spoke, and his desperate, wild-eyed demeanour had softened into the genial mask of the raconteur. I had the impression that these were stories he had told before and liked to tell, as though he had discovered the power and pleasure of reliving events with their sting removed. The skill, I saw, lay in skirting close enough to what appeared to be the truth without allowing what you actually felt about it to regain its power over you.

I asked him how, given his oath, he had come to find himself on an aeroplane again.

He smiled again somewhat shamefacedly and ran a hand through his fine brown hair.

'My daughter's playing in a music festival over there,' he said. 'She plays for her school orchestra. The – ah – oboe.'

He had been supposed to fly out with his wife and children yesterday but their dog had been taken ill and he'd had to let them go on without him. It might sound ridiculous, but the dog was probably the most important member of their family. He'd had to sit up with him all night and then drive straight to the airport.

'To be honest I shouldn't have been behind the wheel of a car,' he said in a low voice, leaning his elbow on the armrest between us. 'I could hardly see straight. I kept passing these signs by the road with the same words on them over and over again and I started to think they'd been put there for me. You know the ones I mean – they're everywhere. It took me ages to work out what they were. I did wonder,' he said, with his abashed smile, 'if I was actually going mad. I couldn't understand who had chosen them, or why. They seemed to be addressing me personally. Obviously,' he said, 'I read the news, but I've got a bit behind since leaving work.'

I said it was true that the question of whether to leave or remain was one we usually asked ourselves in private, to the extent that it could almost be said to constitute the innermost core of self-determination. If you were unfamiliar with the political situation in our country, you might think you were witnessing not the machinations of a democracy but the final surrender of personal consciousness into the public domain.

'The funny thing is,' the man said, 'it felt as if I'd been asking myself that question for as long as I could remember.'

I asked him what had happened to the dog.

For a moment he looked confused, as though he couldn't remember which dog I was talking about. Then he furrowed his brow and pouted and blew out a great sigh.

'It's a bit of a long story,' he said.

The dog – his name was Pilot – was actually quite old, he said, though you wouldn't have thought it to look at him. He and his wife got Pilot shortly after they were married. They had bought their house in the countryside, he said, and it was an ideal place to have a dog. Pilot was a small puppy, but even then he had the most enormous paws: they knew the breed could get very large, but nothing had prepared them for the extraordinary size to which Pilot eventually grew. Every time they thought he couldn't get any bigger, he did: sometimes it was almost funny to see how disproportionately small he made everything around him look, their house and their car and even one another.

'I'm unusually tall,' he said, 'and sometimes you get sick of being taller than everyone else. But when I stood next to Pilot, I felt normal.'

His wife was pregnant with their first child and so Pilot became his own project: he didn't travel as much for work in those days, and for several months he spent most of his free time training Pilot, walking in the hills with him and forming his character. He never spoiled him or gave in to him; he exercised him unfailingly and rewarded him sparingly, and when, as a young dog, Pilot chased a herd of sheep, he beat him with a severity and with a confidence that surprised even himself. Most of all, he was careful how he behaved in front of Pilot, for all the world as if the dog were human, and indeed by the time he reached maturity Pilot possessed an unusual intelligence, as well as a ferocious bark and a giant, muscular body. He treated the family with a sensitivity and consideration that other people found frankly uncanny, though over time they themselves had become used to it. For instance, when their son was seriously ill with pneumonia last year, Pilot had sat outside his room day and night and automatically came to get them if the child called for anything. He was attuned to and even mirrored their daughter's periodic episodes of depression, which sometimes they had only become aware of because Pilot had grown morose and withdrawn.

Yet if a stranger came to the house he would trans-form himself into a guard dog of the utmost vigilance and ruthlessness. People who didn't know him were terrified of him, and rightly, because he would have killed them without hesitation if they had presented any threat to the members of the household.

It was when Pilot was three or four years old, the man went on, that he got his major career break and began to be away from home for extended periods of time, and he felt able to leave, knowing that the family would be safe in his absences. Sometimes, he said, when he was away, he would think of the dog and feel almost closer to him than to any other living thing. So he couldn't have left him in his own hour of need, despite the fact that his daughter was to be the main soloist at the concert and had been practising for weeks. The performance was part of an international festival and there would be a large audience: it was a fantastic opportunity. Yet Betsy didn't want to let Pilot out of her sight. He had the devil's own job getting her to go: it was as if she didn't trust him to look after his own dog.

I asked what piece she was playing and he ruffled his hair again.

'I'm not actually sure,' he said. 'Her mother would know, obviously.'

He hadn't really realised his daughter was so good

at playing the oboe, he added. She had started taking lessons when she was six or seven and frankly it had always sounded pretty awful, to the extent that he had had to ask her to do it in her room. The squeaking noise set his teeth on edge, particularly when he'd come off a long flight. Often he could still hear the reedy, insinuating sound behind her closed door and if he was trying to sleep off his jet lag it was actually quite annoying. He had wondered once or twice whether she did it to persecute him, but apparently she practised just as much when he wasn't there. Occasionally he had gone so far as to suggest that it might be healthier for her to practise less and do other things more, but this opinion had been met with much the same scorn as his attempts to impose discipline on the family timetable. And to be honest, when asked what he thought she ought to be doing with her time, all he could think of were the kinds of things he'd done at her age – socialising and watching television – that he somehow considered more normal. As far as he was concerned, hardly anything about Betsy was normal. For example, she suffered from insomnia: what average fourteen-year-old can't sleep? Instead of eating dinner, she would stand by the kitchen cupboards lifting handfuls of dry cereal to her mouth straight from the box. She never went outside and, since her mother drove her everywhere, rarely walked. He had been told that when he wasn't there she walked Pilot every day, but since he never witnessed it he found it difficult to believe. It had got to the point where he'd started to wonder how she was ever going to leave home, and whether they might have to keep her there forever, like some kind of failed experiment.

Then one evening Betsy was playing in a school concert and he went along with his wife, and with every expectation of being secretly bored sat jammed into a small chair in the auditorium amidst the other parents. The lights came up and in front of the orchestra on the stage stood a girl he took a long time to recognise as Betsy. She seemed much older, for a start; and there was something else, perhaps the fact that she didn't appear to need him or to reproach him with the problem of her existence, that was startlingly reliev-ing. Once he accepted that it was her, what he felt was the most terrible, ominous fear. He was absolutely certain she would embarrass herself and he clutched his wife's hand, believing she felt the same way. The conductor arrived – a man he immediately prepared himself to dislike, dressed in black jeans and a black polo-neck sweater – and the orchestra began to play, and at a certain point Betsy started playing too. What he noticed was how closely Betsy watched this con-ductor and responded to his slightest sign, nodding her head and lifting the instrument to her lips, her large eyes unblinking. Of such a silent feat of intimacy and obedience he had not thought his daughter capable, he who couldn't persuade her to eat her cereal from a bowl. Only after some minutes did he connect the eerie, snaking sound with her more literally: he had sat in enough audiences to know that this one was charmed, spellbound, and only then was he able to really listen. What he heard drew water from his eyes in such quantities that people began to glance round at him in their seats. Afterwards Betsy claimed she could see him weeping from the stage because of his height. She said it had been embarrassing.

I asked him why he thought he had cried, and his mouth tugged unexpectedly downwards in the corners so that he tried to hide it with his large hand.

'To be honest,' he said, 'I suppose I'd always worried there was something wrong with her.'

I said it seemed to me people often found it easier to entertain that idea about their children than about themselves, and he looked at me as though he were momentarily considering that theory before firmly shaking his head.

From earliest childhood, he said, Betsy had been unlike other children – and not in a good way. She was unbelievably neurotic: when they went to the beach, for example, she couldn't bear the feeling of sand under her feet and so they would have to carry her everywhere. She couldn't stand the sounds of certain words and would scream and put her hands over her ears if anyone said them. The list of things she wouldn't eat, and the reasons why, was so long it was impossible to keep up with. She was allergic to everything and constantly ill and was also, as he'd said, an insomniac. Often he and his wife would wake in the middle of the night to find Betsy standing beside their bed like a ghost in her nightdress, staring down at them. As she grew older the most serious problem of all became her extraordinary sensitivity to what she called lying, but what was actually as far as he could see the normal conventions and speech patterns of adult conversation. She claimed that most of what people said was fake and insincere, and when he'd asked her how she could possibly know that, she replied that she could tell by the sound. As he'd said, even as a very small child the sound of certain words had been unbearable to her, but as she got older and started school this problem became more rather than less pronounced. They had moved her to a different school that dealt with her problems more expertly, but even so it made family and social relationships somewhat difficult when their child would run shrieking from the room with her hands clamped to her ears just because one of their guests had claimed to be so full she couldn't possibly eat dessert, or that business was booming despite the economic downturn. He and his wife had tried hard to understand their daughter, to the extent that when they talked to each other after the children had gone to bed they would try to inculcate her sensitivity in themselves, straining their ears to hear the insincerity in one another's phrases, and they had discovered that it was indeed true that much of what you said was pretty scripted and that if you really thought about it you could admit it didn't often represent how you actually felt. But they still fell foul of Betsy with great regularity, and he had noticed that his wife was growing increasingly silent, which he believed to be Betsy's doing, by creating such a minefield around communication that it was easier to say nothing at all.

Perhaps for this reason – because he couldn't speak, and therefore lie – Betsy adored Pilot with a sometimes unnerving ferocity. Yet not long ago there had been an episode that had caused him to question, for the first time, Betsy's definition of truth and her tyranny in the matter of storytelling. He had taken her out with him to walk Pilot and the dog had suddenly bolted. They were in the park of a stately home and somehow he had failed to realise that they kept deer there and had let Pilot off his lead. Usually Pilot was scrupulously obedient around livestock, but on this occasion he had behaved in a way that was completely out of character.

One minute he was there beside them, and the next he was gone.

'You wouldn't believe that animal's speed,' he said. 'He was an enormous dog and when he chose to move there was no way anyone could catch him. He'd lengthen his stride and just change into another gear altogether. He was fifty yards away before we knew it,' he said, 'and we just stood there and watched him flying across the park. When the deer saw him they started to run, although it was already far too late for them to escape. There must have been hundreds of them. I don't know whether you've ever seen anything like that,' he said, 'but in an awful way it's a beautiful sight. They run in a body, like water. We watched them streaming over the park with Pilot on their heels and despite everything I was almost mesmerised by it. They kept turning and doubling back in a big figure of eight and he followed them but it was almost as if he was steering them, making them describe some pattern he already had in his head. For about five minutes they carried on like that, round and round in these big flowing lines, and then suddenly it was as if he got bored or decided it needed to end. Completely effortlessly he just doubled his speed and he penetrated the body of the herd and he picked off one of the young ones and he brought it down. There was this woman standing near us,' he said, 'and she started screaming at us and saying she was going to report us and get someone to come and shoot him, and I was trying to calm her down and we suddenly heard this noise behind us and we look round and Betsy has fainted. She's lying there out cold on the grass and there's blood coming from her head where she hit a stone as she fell. Honestly,' he said, 'she looked like she was dead. Pilot had taken off into the woods by this point and the woman was so worried about Betsy that she forgot about shooting the dog and helped me carry her to the car and came with us all the way to the hospital. Betsy was fine, of course.'

He laughed grimly and shook his head.

I asked him what happened to the dog.

'Oh, he came back that night,' he said. 'I heard him at the door and when I opened it he didn't come in but just stood there outside looking at me. He was absolutely filthy and covered in blood and he knew what was coming to him. He expected it. I hated beating him though,' he said sadly. 'I only had to do it two or three times in his life. We both knew he couldn't have been what he was without it. But Betsy refused to accept what he had done. She wouldn't touch him or speak to him for weeks. She wouldn't speak to me either. She just didn't get it at all. I said to her, you know, you don't train a dog by sulking and being in a mood with him. You'll just make him sly and dishonest.

You know, I said to her, the reason you feel safe when I'm not here is because you know that if anyone tried to hurt any of you, Pilot would do to them what he did to that deer. He might sit on the sofa with you and bring you things and lie next to you on the bed when you're ill, but when someone he doesn't know knocks at the door he's ready to kill them if need be. He's an animal, I said, and he needs to be disciplined, but when you impose your sensitivities on him you interfere with his nature.'

He was silent for a while, his chin lifted, staring down the grey aisle where the air hostess was pushing her trolley through the sea of people. She turned to left and right, bending from the waist across the rows, the lifted corners of her eyes and mouth so sharply delineated that they almost seemed to have been intricately carved out of the smooth oval of her head. Her automatic movements were hypnotising and the man appeared to go into a kind of daze watching her. After a while his head began to nod forward until it fell with such a jolt that he sat up again.

'Sorry,' he said.

He rubbed his face energetically, and after staring past me out of the window for a while and breathing deeply through his nose, he asked me whether I had ever been to this part of Europe before.

I told him I had gone there only once, years ago,

with my son. He was finding life difficult at the time, I said, and I had thought a trip away would be good for him. But then at the last minute I had decided to take another boy along too, the son of a friend of mine. My friend was ill and needed to go to hospital and so I thought it would help her. The two boys didn't get on very well, I said, and my friend's son needed a lot of attention, so while my own son might have expected to be my focus for a few days, in the end it didn't work out like that. There was an exhibition I very much wanted to see and so one morning I persuaded the two of them to come with me to the gallery. I had thought we could walk there but I had judged the distances wrongly and we ended up walking for miles along a sort of motorway in the pouring rain. It turned out my friend's son never went to galleries and wasn't interested in art, and he began to misbehave, so that the attendants had to reprimand him and eventually asked him to leave. In the end I had to sit with him in the café in our wet clothes while my son went to the exhibition on his own. He was gone for about an hour, I said, and when he came back he described everything he'd seen for me. I didn't know, I said, whether it was ever possible to ascribe a final value to the experience of parenthood, to ever see it in its totality, but that time we spent in the café while he talked was one of its moments of grace. One of the things he'd seen was a giant wooden crate in which the artist had reconstructed his own room in its life-sized entirety. Everything was there – furniture, clothes, typewriter, piles of paper and books lying open on the desk, dirty coffee cups – but it had been inverted so that the floor was the ceiling and the whole room was upside down. My son had been particularly struck by this upside-down room, which you entered through a small doorway in the crate, and had spent a long time inside it. Often, I said, in the years afterwards, I would remember his description of it and imagine him sitting there, in a world that contains all the same elements but is the other way round from how you expect it to be.

The man was listening with an expression of mild puzzlement on his face.

'And did he go on to become an artist?' he said, as though that could be the only explanation for my telling him these things.

He would be going to university in the autumn, I said, to study art history.

'Oh, okay,' he said, nodding his head.

His own son, he said, was the academic type, far more so than Betsy. He wanted to be a vet. He kept all sorts of weird animals in his room: a chinchilla, a snake, a pair of rats. They had a friend who was a vet and his son spent most of his weekends there, at the

24

surgery. It was his son, in fact, who had noticed there was something wrong with Pilot. The dog had been very quiet and subdued for the past couple of weeks. They had put it down to his age, but then one evening his son was fondling Pilot and noticed a swelling in his side. A couple of days later, when his wife was out and the children were at school, he took Pilot to his vet friend, not really thinking anything of it. The vet examined him and said that Pilot had cancer.

He paused and looked past me out of the window again.

'I didn't really know dogs could have cancer,' he said. 'I'd never thought about how Pilot would die. I asked whether he could operate and he said there was no point – it was too far gone. So he gave him some drugs for the pain and I drove him home again. All the way home,' he said, 'I kept seeing Pilot as he was when he was young and strong and powerful. I thought about all the years he had been here while I was away for weeks at a time, and the fact that he was fading now that I had retired seemed significant somehow. Most of all I dreaded telling the others, because to be honest I'm not sure they wouldn't rather have had Pilot than me. I started to feel I had upset everything by coming home. They had all seemed so happy when I wasn't there, and now my wife and I were arguing all the time and the kids were shouting and slamming doors and to top it all,' he said, 'I'd caused the dog to get ill, when he'd never shown a second of weakness his whole life. Anyway,' he said, 'I did tell them, though admittedly I made it sound less serious than it was. We had arranged for him to go to kennels while we were abroad but I knew he wouldn't make it, so I told them to go on without me. They were pretty suspicious. They made me promise to phone them if he got worse so that they could come back. They even called that evening from the hotel and made me swear I wouldn't let Pilot die while they were away. I said he was okay and that it was just a cold or something and that he'd probably be fine in the morning.' He paused and looked at me sideways. 'I didn't even tell my wife.'

I asked him why not and he paused again.

'When she was giving birth to the kids she didn't want me to be there,' he said. 'I remember her saying she wouldn't be able to handle the pain if I was in the room. She had to do it on her own. They loved Pilot,' he said, 'but it was me who had trained him and disciplined him and made him what he was. In a sense I created him,' he said, 'to stand in for me when I wasn't there. I don't think anyone could have understood what I felt about him, not even them. And the idea of them being there and of their feelings having to take priority over mine was pretty unbearable, which I think,' he said, 'was more or less what she meant.

'Anyway,' he went on, 'Pilot had this big bed in the kitchen where he used to sleep and he was lying there stretched out on his side and so I went and got some cushions and I made him as comfortable as I could and I sat down next to him on the floor. He was panting very fast and he was looking at me with these huge, sad eyes and for a long time we just stayed there, looking at each other. I stroked his head and talked to him and he lay there panting and at around midnight I started to wonder how long this was going to go on for. I didn't really know anything about the dying process – I've never been with someone when they died – and I realised I was beginning to feel impatient. It wasn't even that I wanted him to get it over with for his own sake. I just wanted something to happen. For pretty much my whole adult life,' he said, 'I've been on my way somewhere or on my way back. I've never been in any situation without the prospect of it ending or of having to leave at a set time and even though that way of living was sometimes unpleasant, in a sense I'd become addicted to it. At the same time I was thinking about how people say you should put animals out of their misery, and I wondered whether what I ought to be doing was knocking him out or putting a pillow over his face and whether I was just

27

too weak or scared. And it felt weirdly like Pilot would have known the answer to that question. In the end at about two in the morning I cracked and called the vet and he said that if I wanted him to, he would come straight over and give him an injection. So I asked him what would happen if we just left it as it was and he said he didn't know – it could be hours or it could be days or even weeks. It's up to you, he said. So I said to him, look, is the dog dying or not? And he said yes, of course he's dying, but it's a mysterious process and you can either wait it out or you can choose to bring it to an end. And then I started to think about Betsy playing in her concert the next day and about how tired I'd be and all the things I had to do and so I told him to come over. And he was there fifteen minutes later.'

I asked him what happened in those fifteen minutes.

'Nothing,' he said. 'Nothing at all. I was still sitting there and Pilot was still panting and gazing at me with these big eyes and I didn't feel anything particularly, just that I was waiting for someone to come and get me out of this situation. It felt like it had become false, yet now,' he said, 'I would give literally anything to be back in it, to be back in that room in that precise moment of time.

'Eventually the vet came and it was very quick and he closed Pilot's eyes and gave me a number to call in the morning for someone to come and take the body away, and then he left. So there I was in the same room with the same dog, only now the dog was dead. I started to think about what my wife and kids would say if they knew, if they could see me sitting there, and I realised then that I had done something awful, something they would never have done, something so cowardly and unnatural and now so completely irreversible that it felt like I would never, ever get over it and that things would never be the same again. And in a way it was just to hide the evidence of what I'd done that I decided to bury him then and there. I went out to the shed in the dark and got a spade and then I chose a place in the garden and I started to dig. And all the time I was digging I couldn't tell whether what I was doing was manly and honourable or just fake as well, because at the same time as I was digging I was imagining telling people about it. I was imagining them thinking about my physical strength and my decisiveness, but in fact it was much harder work than I had expected. At the beginning I thought I wasn't going to be able to do it. Yet I knew there was absolutely no way I could give up. I could see how it would look in daylight, me sitting there with a dead dog and a half-dug mess in the garden. The ground was incredibly hard and the spade kept hitting rocks and the hole had to be pretty big to fit Pilot in it. Once or twice I thought I was going to have to admit defeat. Yet after a while,' he said, 'I started to feel that this actually was what it was like to be a man. I realised that I felt anger, and that it was anger that was giving me the strength to do it and so I let myself get angrier and angrier until in the end I wasn't even afraid of what the family would say because they hadn't had to kill the dog and then dig this hole to bury him in. One of the phrases my wife had started to use when we argued about the way she ran things was: "You weren't here". I always hated it, but now I could imagine saying it back to her. I realised how angry she must have been to say it and suddenly I was glad that Pilot was dead. I was actually glad, because it felt like without him we were going to have to admit what we truly felt.'

He paused, an expression of bewilderment on his face.

'I finished digging the hole,' he went on after a while, 'and I went back into the house and I wrapped Pilot in a blanket. I picked him up from his bed and he was so unbelievably heavy I almost dropped him. It would have been easier to drag him,' he said, 'but I knew I couldn't let myself do that because I was already starting to become frightened of the body. When I went back into the house and saw him lying there dead,' he said, 'I had the most unbelievable urge to run away. I had to believe it was still Pilot,' he said, 'or I couldn't have gone through with it. In the end I had to hold him right against my chest,' he said, 'and even then I managed to bang his head on the door frame on my way out, and I was talking to him and apologising to him out loud and somehow I staggered outside with him and got him across the garden and put him in the hole. It was starting to get light. I arranged him all nicely, then I went back inside and got some of his things from his bed and put them down there with him. Then I filled the hole with earth and tided it and marked the edges with stones. Then I went and packed my bag and had a shower. I was absolutely filthy,' he said. 'I had to throw away my shirt. Then I got in the car and drove to the airport.'

He spread out his large hands in front of him and examined them back and front. They were clean, except for the dark, compacted half-moons of dirt under the nails. He looked at me.

'The only thing I couldn't get out was the mud under my fingernails,' he said.

The hotel was completely round: it had at one time been a water tower, the receptionist said, and the repurposing of the building had won the architect many prizes. She gave me a map of the city, smoothing it out across the reception desk with slender, highly varnished fingernails.

'We are here,' she said, circling the spot with a pen.

In the lobby a number of thick pillars ascended through the core of the building, from which walkways extended overhead like the spokes of a wheel. Behind one of these pillars a girl in a T-shirt printed with the festival logo sat at a desk piled with information leaflets. She went through her sheaf of papers, trying to find my details. I was scheduled to participate in an event this afternoon, she said, and after that she believed an interview had been arranged for me with one of the national daily newspapers. The event would take place here in the hotel. In the evening there was a party at a venue in the city centre where food would be provided. The festival was operating a coupon system for food: I could use these coupons both here at the hotel and later at the party. She produced a wad of printed slips, several of which she carefully tore away along a perforated line and handed to me, after making a note of their serial numbers on the list in front of her. She also handed me an information leaflet and a message from my publisher, saying he would meet me before the afternoon event in the hotel bar.

Part of the hotel bar had been cordoned off for a wedding reception. People stood in the dark, low-ceilinged space holding glasses of champagne. The windows along the rounded wall let in a strong, cold light from one side and the contrast of light and dark gave the guests' clothes and faces a slightly garish appearance. A photographer was leading people in pairs or small groups out on to the terrace where they stood in the cool, breezy day, holding their expressions for the camera. The bride and groom were talking and laughing in a circle of guests, side by side but turned away from one another. Their faces wore an expression of self-consciousness, almost of culpability. I noticed that everyone there was around the same age as the married couple, and the absence of anyone older or younger made it seem as though these events were bound neither to the future nor the past, and that no one was entirely certain whether it was freedom or irresponsibility that had untethered them.

The rest of the bar was empty except for a small fairhaired man who sat in a leather booth with a book on the table in front of him. When he saw me he held it up so that I could see its cover. He looked at the back jacket and then looked at me and then looked at it again.

'You are nothing like your photograph!' he exclaimed reproachfully, when I was close enough to hear.

I pointed out that the photograph he had chosen for the cover was more than fifteen years old.

'But I love it!' he said. 'You look so – guileless.'

He began to tell me about another of his authors, whose book photograph showed a slim and lovely woman with a long, fair waterfall of shining hair. In the flesh she was grey-haired and somewhat overweight and unfortunately suffered from an eye condition that obliged her to wear glasses with thick bottle-like lenses. When she appeared at readings and festivals the contrast was most obvious, and he had occasionally raised the delicate question of using a more recent photograph, but she wouldn't hear of it. Why should her photograph be accurate? So that she could be identified by the police? The whole point of her profession, she said, was that it represented an escape from reality. Besides, she preferred being that sylph with the waterfall of hair. In some part of herself, she believed that that was who she still was. A degree of self-deception, she said, was an essential part of the talent for living.

'She is one of our most popular authors,' he said, 'as you can imagine.'

He asked me how I liked the hotel and I said that I had found its circularity surprisingly confusing. Several times already I had tried to go somewhere and found myself back where I started. I hadn't realised, I said, how much of navigation is the belief in progress, and the assumption of fixity in what you have left behind. I had walked around the entire circumference of the building in search of things I had been right next to in the first place, an error that was virtually guaranteed by the fact that all the building's sources of natural

34

light had been concealed by angled partitions, so that the routes around it were almost completely dark. You found the light, in other words, not by following it but by stumbling on it randomly and at greater or lesser length; or to put it another way, you knew where you were only once you had arrived. I didn't doubt that it was for such metaphors that the architect had won his numerous prizes, but it rested on the assumption that people lacked problems of their own, or at the very least had nothing better to do with their time. My publisher widened his eyes.

'For that matter,' he said, 'you could say the same thing about novels.'

He was a delicate-looking man, dapperly dressed in a blazer and striped shirt, with neatly slicked-back flaxen hair and angular silver-framed glasses and a smell of ironing and cologne. His slightness made him seem even younger than he was. He was very fair-skinned – the flesh at the cuffs and collar of his shirt was so white and unmarked it almost looked like plastic – and his pale-pink mouth was as small and soft as a child's mouth. He had been occupying his senior position in the firm for eighteen months, he said now: before that, he had worked on the marketing side of things. Certain people had expressed surprise that one of the country's oldest and most distinguished literary houses should be put in the hands of a thirty-five-year-old salesman, but since he had taken it in that short time from the brink of insolvency to what looked set to be the most profitable year in the company's long history, the critics had one by one fallen silent.

He wore a faint smile while he spoke, and his light-blue eyes behind their glasses glittered with the diffidence of light glittering on water.

'For example,' he said, 'only a year ago I would not have been able to sanction our investment in a work such as this one.' He held up the book with my photograph on it, in what was either accusation or triumph. 'The sad fact,' he said, 'is that in that period even some of our most illustrious writers found themselves for the first time in decades having their manuscripts rejected. There was a great groaning,' he said, smiling, 'as of afflicted beasts bellowing from the tar pit. Certain people could not accept that what they regarded as their entitlement to have whatever they chose to write – whether or not others wished to read it – put into print year after year had been questioned. Unfortunately,' he said, lightly touching the thin steel frame of his glasses, 'there was in some cases a loss of courtesy and control.'

I asked him what, besides the jettisoning of unprofitable literary novels, explained the company's return to solvency, and his smile widened.

'Our biggest success has been with Sudoku,' he said. 'In fact I have become quite addicted to it myself. Obviously there was an outcry that we should be sullying our hands in that way. But I found that it died down quite quickly, once those less popular authors realised it meant their work could be published again.'

What all publishers were looking for, he went on – the holy grail, as it were, of the modern literary scene – were those writers who performed well in the market while maintaining a connection to the values of literature; in other words, who wrote books that people could actually enjoy without feeling in the least demeaned by being seen reading them. He had managed to secure quite a collection of those writers, and apart from the Sudoku and the popular thrillers, they were chiefly responsible for the upswing in the company's fortunes.

I said I was struck by his observation that the preservation of literary values – in however nominal a form – was a factor in the achievement of popular success. In England, I said, people liked to live in old houses that had been thoroughly refurbished with modern conveniences, and I wondered whether the same principle might be applied to novels; and if so, whether the blunting or loss of our own instinct for beauty was responsible for it. An expression of delight came over his fine, white-skinned face and he raised his finger in the air.

'People enjoy combustion!' he exclaimed.

In fact, he went on, you could see the whole history of capitalism as a history of combustion, not just the burning of substances that have lain in the earth for millions of years but also of knowledge, ideas, culture and indeed beauty – anything, in other words, that has taken time to develop and accrue.

'It may be time itself,' he exclaimed, 'that we are burning. For example, take the English writer Jane Austen: I have observed the way in which, over the space of a few years, the novels of this long-dead spinster were used up,' he said, 'burned one after another as spin-offs and sequels, films, self-help books, and even, I believe, a reality TV show. Despite the meagre facts of her life, even the author herself has finally been consumed on the pyre of popular biography. Whether or not it looks like preservation,' he said, 'it is in fact the desire to use the essence until every last drop of it is gone. Miss Austen made a good fire,' he said, 'but in the case of my own successful authors it is the concept of literature itself that is being combusted.'

There was, he added, a generalised yearning for the ideal of literature, as for the lost world of childhood, whose authority and reality tended to seem so much greater than that of the present moment. Yet to return to that reality even for a day would for most people be intolerable, as well as impossible: despite our nostalgia for the past and for history, we would quickly find ourselves unable to live there for reasons of discomfort, since the defining motivation of the modern era, he said, whether consciously or not, is the pursuit of freedom from strictures or hardships of any kind.

'What is history other than memory without pain?' he said, smiling pleasantly and folding his small white hands together on the table in front of him. 'If people want to recapture some of those hardships, these days they go to the gym.'

Similarly, he went on, to experience the nuances of literature without the hard work involved in reading, say, Robert Musil, was for a number of people very pleasurable. For instance, as an adolescent he had read a great deal of poetry, particularly the poetry of T. S. Eliot, yet if he were to pick up the *Four Quartets* today he didn't doubt it would cause him pain, not only because of Eliot's pessimistic view of life but also because it would force him to re-enter the world in which he had first read those poems in all its unvarnished reality. Not everyone, of course, spends their teenage years reading Eliot, he said, but it would be hard to pass through the education system without at some point having to grapple with one antiquated text or another, and so for most people the act of reading symbolised intelligence, quite possibly because in that formative time they had not enjoyed or understood the books that they were obliged to read. It even had connotations of moral virtue and superiority, to the extent that parents worried there was something wrong with their children if they didn't read, yet these parents had quite possibly hated studying literature themselves. Indeed, as he had said, it might even be their forgotten suffering at the hands of literary texts that had left behind this residue of respect for books; if, that is, psychoanalysts are to be believed when they say we are unconsciously drawn to the repetition of painful experiences. And so a cultural product that reproduced that ambiguous attraction, while making no demands and inflicting no pain in the service of it, was bound to succeed. The explosion of book clubs and reading groups and websites overflowing with reader reviews showed no sign of dying down, because the flames were constantly being fed anew by a reverse kind of snobbery that his most successful writers thoroughly understood.

'More than anything,' he said, 'people dislike being made to feel stupid, and if you arouse those feelings, you do so at your own cost. I, for example, like to play tennis,' he said, 'and I know that if I play with someone who is a little better than me, my game will be raised. But if my tennis partner is too far beyond me in skill, he becomes my tormentor and my game is destroyed.'

Sometimes, he said, he amused himself by trawling some of the lower depths of the internet, where readers gave their opinions of their literary purchases, much as they might rate the performance of a detergent. What he had learned, by studying these opinions, was that respect for literature was very much skin deep, and that people were never far from the capacity to abuse it. It was entertaining, in a way, to see Dante awarded a single star out of a possible five and his *Divine Comedy* described as 'complete shit', but a sensitive person might equally find it distressing, until you remembered that Dante – along with most great writers – carved his vision out of the deepest understanding of human nature and could look after himself. It was a position of weakness, he believed, to see literature as something fragile that needed defending, as so many of his colleagues and contemporaries did. Likewise he didn't set much store by its morally beneficial qualities, other than to raise the game – as he had said – of someone correspondingly slightly inferior.

He sat back in his seat and looked at me with a pleasant smile.

I said that I found his remarks somewhat cynical, as well as strikingly indifferent to the concept of justice, whose mysteries, while remaining opaque to us, it had always seemed sensible to me to fear. In fact the very opacity of those mysteries, I said, was in itself grounds for terror, for if the world seemed full of people living evilly without reprisal and living virtuously without reward, the temptation to abandon personal morality might arise in exactly the moment when personal morality is most significant. Justice, in other words, was something you had to honour for its own sake, and whether or not he believed that Dante could look after himself, it seemed to me he ought to defend him at every opportunity.

While I was speaking my publisher had been stealthily removing his eyes from my face in order to look at something over my shoulder, and I turned to see a woman standing at the entrance to the bar gazing around herself nonplussed with her hand shading her eyes, like a voyager peering into foreign distances.

'Ah!' he said. 'There's Linda.'

He waved at her and she gave a jerky gesture of relief as though she had been struggling to find us, though in fact we were the only people there.

'I went to the basement by mistake,' she said when she reached our table. 'There's a garage down there. There are all these cars sitting there in rows. It was horrible.'

The publisher laughed.

'It wasn't funny,' Linda said. 'I felt like I was in

something's lower intestine. The building was digesting me.'

'We are publishing Linda's first novel,' he said, to me. 'The reviews so far have been very encouraging.'

She was a tall, soft, thick-limbed woman made even taller by the elaborately strappy high-heeled sandals she wore on her feet, whose glamour sat incongruously beneath the black tentlike garment she wore and her general air of awkwardness. Her hair was dishevelled and fell past her shoulders in matted-looking hanks, and her skin had the pastiness of someone who rarely goes outdoors. She had a round, loose, somewhat startled face and her mouth hung open while she looked in amazement through large red-framed glasses at the wedding party on the other side of the bar.

'What's that?' she said in puzzlement. 'Are they making a film?'

The publisher explained that the hotel was a popular venue for weddings.

'Oh,' she said. 'I thought it was a joke or something.'

She slumped down heavily in the booth, fanning her face and plucking at the neck of her black garment with the other hand.

'We were just talking about Dante,' the publisher said pleasantly.

Linda stared at him.

'Were we meant to have studied that for today?' she said.

He laughed loudly.

'The only topic is yourself,' he said. 'That's what people are paying to hear about.'

We both listened while he gave us the details of the event in which we were participating. He would introduce us, he said, and then there would be a few minutes of conversation, before the readings began, in which he would ask each of us two or three questions about ourselves.

'But you already know the answers, right?' Linda said.

It was a formality, he said, just to allow everyone to relax.

'Ice-breaking,' Linda said. 'I'm familiar with the concept. I like a little ice in things though,' she added. 'I just prefer it that way.'

She talked about a reading she had done in New York with a well-known novelist. They had agreed beforehand how the reading would go, but when they got on stage the novelist announced to the audience that instead of reading they were going to sing. The audience went wild for this idea and the novelist stood up and sang.

The publisher roared with laughter and clapped his hands so that Linda jumped.

'Sang what?' he said.

'I don't know,' Linda said. 'Some kind of Irish folk tune.'

'And what did you sing?' he said.

'It was the worst thing that's ever happened to me,' Linda said.

The publisher was smiling and shaking his head.

'Genius,' he said.

Another reading she did was with a poet, Linda said. The poet was a kind of cult figure and the audience was huge. The poet's boyfriend always participated in her public performances, going around the audience while she read, sitting on people's laps or fondling them. On this occasion he had brought with him a giant ball of string and he had crawled up and down the rows, looping the string around their ankles so that by the end the whole audience was tied together.

The publisher gave another roar of laughter.

'You must read Linda's novel,' he said, to me. 'It's quite hilarious.'

Linda looked at him, quizzical and unsmiling.

'It isn't meant to be,' she said.

'But that is exactly why people here love it!' he said. 'It reassures them of the absurdity of life, without causing them to feel that they themselves are absurd. In your stories you are always the – what is the word?'

'The butt,' Linda said flatly. 'Is it hot in here?' she added. 'I'm stifling. It's probably the menopause,' she said, and made quotation marks in the air with her fingers: 'Ice melts as woman writer overheats.'

This time the publisher did not laugh, but merely looked at her with bright neutrality, his eyes unblinking behind their glasses.

'I've been on tour so long I'm starting to pass through the stages of ageing,' she said to me. 'My face hurts from having to smile all the time. I've eaten all this weird food and now this dress is the only thing I can fit into. I've worn it so many times it's become like my apartment.'

I asked her where she'd been before coming here and she said she had gone to France, Spain and the UK, and before that had spent two weeks at a writers' retreat in Italy. The retreat was in a castle on a hill in the middle of nowhere. For a place promoting solitary contemplation, it was pretty hectic. It belonged to a countess who liked to spend her dead husband's money on surrounding herself with writers and artists. In the evenings you were expected to sit at the dinner table with her and supply stimulating conversation. The countess selected and invited the writers personally: most of them were young and male. In fact there was only one other woman writer there besides Linda.

'I'm fat and forty,' Linda said, 'and the other one was gay, so you can go figure.'

One of the writers, a young black poet, had escaped on the second day. The countess had been particularly proud of capturing this poet: she boasted about him to anyone who would listen. When he announced his intention of leaving she went wild, alternately begging and demanding an explanation, but he was unmoved by her distress. It was not the right place for him, he said. He was not comfortable there and would not be able to work. And he had packed his bag and walked the three miles down into the village to get a bus, since the countess refused to help him by ordering a taxi. She had spent the rest of the two weeks coldly savaging him and his work to anyone who would listen. Linda had watched him disappear off down the long winding drive from her room. He walked with a light, bouncing stride, carrying his small knapsack over his shoulder. She very much wanted to do the same thing, while knowing at the same time that she couldn't. The reason appeared to be the enormous size of her suitcase. Also, she wasn't sure she could have walked three miles in her shoes. Instead she had sat in her antique-filled room with its beautiful view of the valley and whenever she looked at her watch, believing that an hour had passed, she would find that barely ten minutes had.

'I couldn't write a word,' she said. 'I couldn't even read. There was this antique telephone on the desk and I kept wanting to call someone up and get them to come and rescue me. One day I finally picked it up and it wasn't connected – it was just a decoration.'

The publisher let out a brief, high-pitched giggle.

'But why should they rescue you?' he said. 'There you are, sitting in a castle in the beautiful Italian countryside, with your own room and nobody bothering you and complete freedom to do your work. For most people that is a fantasy!'

'I don't know,' Linda said dully. 'I guess it must mean there's something wrong with me.'

Her room in the castle was full of paintings and exquisite leather-bound books and costly rugs, she went on, and the linen on the bed was luxurious. Every last detail was in perfect taste and it was all scrupulously clean and polished and scented. After a while she realised that the only imperfect thing in it was herself.

'Our whole apartment could have fitted into that one room,' she said. 'There was this big wooden wardrobe and I kept opening it thinking I might find my husband living in there, spying on me through the keyhole. But in the end,' she said, 'I guess I sort of wanted to find him in there.'

There was a terrace with a beautiful swimming pool

right underneath her window but she never saw any-one swim in it. There were loungers placed around it and if you went and lay on one, a servant would automatically come out and bring you a drink on a tray. She had witnessed this mechanism several times without testing it herself.

'Why not?' the publisher said amusedly.

'If I went out there and lay down and the servant didn't come out,' Linda said, 'it would have meant something terrible.'

Every morning the countess would emerge in her gold wrapper and lie on one of the loungers among the flowers in the sun. She would open her wrapper and reveal her skinny brown body and she would lie there like a lizard, sunbathing. After a few minutes one of the other writers would always walk past, as if by chance. Whoever it was would talk to the count-ess, sometimes for a long time. From her room Linda would hear the sound of them talking and laughing. These other writers, she went on, mocked the count-ess behind her back in discreet and witty ways that left no evidence that could be used later against them. Whether this was because they loved her or because they hated her Linda couldn't tell, but after a while she realised it was neither. They didn't love or hate any-thing, or at least so that you could see; it was just that they were in the habit of never showing their hand.

At mealtimes the countess would take only the tiniest bites of the food, and then she would light a cigarette and smoke it very slowly before stubbing it out in her plate. She dressed for dinner in gowns that were tight and low-cut and she was always dripping with jewellery – gold and diamonds and pearls – on her arms and fingers and around her throat, as well as suspended from her ears, so that she made a centre of light in the shadowy dining room. It was impossible, in other words, to be unaware of her: she would watch the people around the table with a rapt, glittering, hawk-eyed expression, prowling the conversation like a predator monitoring its hunting-ground. Because they were conscious of her, everyone made an effort to say witty and interesting things. Yet because she didn't conceal herself the conversation was never real: it was the conversation of people imitating writers having a conversation, and the morsels she fed on were lifeless and artificial, as well as being laid directly at her feet, so that the spectacle of her satisfaction was artificial too. They all worked hard at this contrivance, Linda said, which was puzzling because she couldn't see what any of them were actually getting out of it. The countess, she added, wore her hair piled so high on her head that it made her neck seem exceptionally fragile, so that you felt you could reach out and snap it in two with your hands.

At this remark the publisher gave an alarmed shout of laughter and Linda looked at him expressionlessly.

'I didn't actually snap it,' she said.

Those mealtimes were a torture, she resumed presently, not just because of what she now realised was their atmosphere of mutual prostitution, but also because she felt so tense that her stomach was one big knot and she couldn't eat the food. In fact she probably ate even less than the countess herself, and one evening the countess turned to her, her coruscating eyes open in wonder, and expressed surprise that Linda was so large, since she ate so little.

'I thought she might be angry about it,' Linda said, 'because the maid was having to take away my plate full of wasted food, but in fact it was the only time she showed any interest in me, as though her idea of friendship with another woman was just sharing moments of self-torture. And in fact whenever the maid came to clear the table or to bring new courses I had to stop myself from getting up and helping her.'

At home she generally avoided doing housework, she went on, because those kinds of chores made her feel so unimportant that she wouldn't have been able to write anything afterwards. She supposed they made her feel like an ordinary woman, when most of the time she didn't think about being a woman, or perhaps didn't even believe she was one, because at

51

home it wasn't a subject that came up. Her husband did most of the domestic work, she said, because he liked doing it and it didn't have the same effect on him that it did on her.

'But in Italy I started to feel that if I did the chores it would justify my existence,' she said. 'I even started to miss my husband. I kept thinking about him and about how critical I always am of him, and increasingly I couldn't remember why I criticised him, because the more I thought about him the more perfect he became in my head. I started to think about our daughter and about how cute and innocent she is, and I completely forgot the fact that being with her sometimes makes me feel like I'm trapped in a room with a swarm of bees. I always fantasised about going on a writing retreat,' she said, 'and being able to sit in the evening and talk to other writers, rather than spending my time in our apartment arguing with my husband and daughter about stupid things. But now all I wanted was to be there again, despite the fact that I'd been counting the days until I could get away. One night I called them,' she said, 'and my husband answered the phone and he sounded just the tiniest bit surprised when I said it was me. We talked for a little while and then there was this silence and eventually he said, what can I do for you?'

The publisher burst out laughing. 'How romantic!' he said.

'So I ask him what's going on over there,' Linda went on, 'and he says, nothing, we're just pootling along. My husband has the habit of using these cutesy English words,' she added. 'It's kind of irritating.'

'So the man you were missing wasn't him,' the publisher said, with a satisfied air of deduction.

'I guess not,' Linda said. 'It kind of brought me to my senses. Suddenly I could see our apartment completely clearly. We were talking on the phone and I could see the stain on the carpet in the hall where one of the garbage bags once leaked and the kitchen where the cupboard doors are all crooked and the bathroom sink that has a crack the exact same shape as Nicaragua,' she said. 'I could even smell the drain smell that there always is in there. Things got better after that,' she said, folding her arms and looking over at the wedding party across the bar. 'I actually had a good time. I had second helpings of pasta every night,' she added. 'It was worth it to see the look on the countess's face. And I admit some of the others turned out to be stimulating, as advertised.'

Still, after two weeks she could see it was possible to have too much of a good thing. There was a man there, a novelist, who was going straight on to another residency in France, and then another one in Sweden after that: his whole life, as far as she could see, consisted of writerly sinecures and engagements, like a whole life of eating only dessert. She wasn't sure it was healthy. But one evening she did get talking to a writer who told her that every day, when he sat down to write, he would think of an object that didn't mean anything to him and would set himself the task of including it somewhere in that day's work. She asked him for examples and he said that in the past few days he had chosen a lawnmower, a fancy wristwatch, a cello and a caged parrot. The cello was the only one that hadn't worked, he said, because he had forgotten when he chose it that his parents had tried to make him learn the cello when he was a child. His mother loved the sound of the cello, but he was terrible at it. The wailing noise he made wasn't what she'd had in mind at all and in the end he gave it up. 'So the story he writes,' Linda said, 'is about some kid who's a cello genius and it's so exaggerated and unbelievable he has to throw it away. The point about these objects, he said, is that they're meant to help him see things as they really are. Anyway,' Linda said, 'I said I would try it because I hadn't written one word since I'd been there, and I ask him to give me something to start me off and he suggests a hamster. You know,' she said, 'the little furry thing in the cage.'

It was true that a hamster meant nothing to her, she said, since they had a no-pets policy in their building, and what she felt straight away was the leverage this rodent gave her in describing the human triangle at home. She'd tried to write about the family dynamic before but somehow, no matter how cold it had come out of the freezer of her heart, it always ended up turning to mush in her hands. The problem, she now saw, was that she had been trying to describe her husband and daughter using materials – her feelings – that no one else could see. The solid fact of the hamster made all the difference. She could describe them petting it and fawning over it while its imprisonment got increasingly on Linda's nerves, and the way it solidified their bond so that Linda felt left out. What kind of love was this, that needed the love object domesticated and locked up? And if there was love being handed out, why wasn't she getting any? It occurred to Linda that since their daughter had found a satisfactory companion in the hamster, her husband might have taken the opportunity to round that situation out by returning his attention to his wife, yet the opposite was the case: he could leave the child alone less than ever. Every time she went near the cage he would leap to his feet to join her, until Linda wondered whether he was actually jealous of the hamster and was only pretending to love it as a way of keeping hold of her. She wondered whether secretly he wanted to kill it, and since she'd realised in the meantime that she felt at best ambivalent about the possibility of him resuming an interest in herself, it became important to her to keep the hamster alive. Sometimes she felt sorry for the hamster as the unwitting victim of the mutual narcissism of human relationships: she had heard that if you put two hamsters in a cage together they would end up killing each other, so they were compelled to live alone. At night she was kept awake by the whirring sound of it running frenziedly on its wheel. In one version, her daughter comes to love the hamster so much that she sets it free. But in the final version it is Linda herself who frees it, opening the cage and shooing it out of the apartment while her daughter is at school. Worse still, she allows her daughter to think that she herself left the cage open by mistake that morning and that she is therefore to blame.

'It's a good story,' Linda said flatly. 'My agent just sold it to *The New Yorker*.'

Still, she wasn't sure quite what she'd gained from her tour, unless it was weight from all the pasta she'd eaten. It had occurred to her that by calling her husband and putting an end to the feeling of being unmoored and adrift she may have missed the opportunity to understand something. She'd been reading a novel by Hermann Hesse, she said, where he describes something similar.

'The character is sitting by this river,' she said, 'just looking at the shapes the dark and light make on the water, and at the weird shapes of what might be fish beneath the surface, there for a second and then gone again, and he realises that he's looking at something he can't describe and that no one could describe using language. And he sort of gets the feeling that what he can't describe might be the true reality.'

'Hesse is completely unfashionable now,' my publisher said with a dismissive flick of his hand. 'It is almost an embarrassment to be seen reading him.'

'I guess that explains why everyone was giving me weird looks on the plane,' Linda said. 'I thought it was because I'd only put make-up on one half of my face. I got to the hotel and looked in the mirror and realised I'd only done one side. Probably the only person who didn't realise was the woman sitting next to me,' she said, 'since she was looking at me sideways and never saw the other half to compare. In any case, she looked pretty strange herself. She told me she just came out of hospital after breaking nearly every bone in her body. She was a skier and she skied over a precipice in a snowstorm. She spent six months being reassembled. They built her out of these metal rods and pinned her together.'

During the flight this woman had recounted the story of her accident, Linda went on, which happened in the Austrian Alps, where the woman was working as a ski guide. She had taken out a group, despite the fact that the forecast was bad, for this group were fanatical skiers and were determined to cover a famously dangerous stretch of off-piste terrain in what were unusually good powder conditions for the time of year. They had urged her to take them, against her better judgement, and she had had ample opportunity during her six months in hospital to consider the extent of their responsibility for what then happened, but in the end she had accepted that no amount of pressure could obscure the fact that the decision had been her own. In fact it was a miracle that none of them had gone over the edge with her, because they were all skiing too fast in their desire to get down before the storm trapped them there. Moments before the accident, the woman said she remembered feeling an extraordinary sense of her own power, and also of her freedom, despite the fact that she knew the mountain could rescind her freedom in an instant. Yet in those moments it suddenly seemed like a childlike game, an opportunity to take leave of reality, and when she went over the precipice and the mountain fell away beneath her, for an instant she almost believed that she could fly. What happened next had to be pieced together from other people's accounts, since she didn't remember it herself, but it seemed the group had not hesitated in continuing down the mountain without her, since they absolutely assumed she couldn't have survived the fall and was dead. Two days later, she had walked into a mountain refuge and collapsed. No one understood how she had been able to walk with so many broken bones; it was an impossibility, yet she had undeniably done it.

'I asked her how she thought it had happened,' Linda said, 'and she said that she simply hadn't known her bones were broken. She didn't even feel any pain. When she said that,' Linda said, 'it suddenly felt like she was talking about me.'

I asked her what she meant and she was silent for so long, slumped back in the booth with an impassive expression on her face, that it seemed she might not answer.

'I guess it reminded me of having a kid,' she said finally. 'You survive your own death,' she added, 'and then there's nothing left to do except talk about it.'

It was hard to explain, she went on, but her feelings of affinity with the metal woman did seem to stem from an experience that for her had likewise been a process of being broken and then reassembled into an indestructible, unnatural and possibly suicidal version of herself. Like she'd said, you survived your own death and there was nothing left to do but talk about it, to strangers on a plane or whoever would listen. Unless you set your heart on finding a new way to die, she said. Skiing over a precipice sounded okay, and she'd thought of paying someone to take her up in an aeroplane just to see if she could resist opening her parachute, but in the end writing was what generally kept her from going down that road. When she wrote she was neither in nor out of her body: she was just ignoring it.

'Like the family dog,' she said. 'You can treat that dog how you like. It's never going to be free, if it even remembers what freedom is.'

We sat looking at the wedding party on the other side of the room, where someone was making a speech while the bride and groom stood side by side smiling. Occasionally the bride would look down to smooth the front of her dress and whenever she looked up again there was an instant before her smile would reappear. We sat watching until a harried-looking girl wearing a festival T-shirt and carrying a clipboard came to the table to tell us the audience was waiting. The publisher slid out of the booth and smoothed the front of his blazer in a gesture that oddly mirrored the bride's. Standing up, Linda towered over him. We followed him out in single file. I noticed how carefully she had to walk in her high-heeled shoes.

I had been told that the interviewer was waiting for me outside in the hotel garden. The muffled oceanic roar of traffic rose steadily from the nearby road. She was sitting alone on a bench amid the raw planted beds and network of gravel paths, gazing down the hill towards the city where the snaking dark shape of the river wound through the old town, trapped by the intricate architecture clamped to its sides. The blackened spikes of the cathedral could be seen jutting above the rooftops.

She had come directly from the train station on foot, she said, since in this city to go anywhere by car was effectively a diversion from one's aims. The post-war road system had been built apparently without thought for the notion of travelling between two points. The giant freeways circled the city without penetrating it, she said: to get anywhere, you had to go everywhere; the roads were permanently jammed while lacking the logic of a common destination. But it was a perfectly pleasant short walk through the centre. She stood up to shake my hand.

'Actually,' she said, 'we've met before.'

I know, I said, and her huge eyes lit up for a second in her gaunt face.

'I wasn't sure you'd remember,' she said.

It had been more than ten years ago yet the encounter had stayed with me, I said. She had described her home and her life in a way that had often returned to me during those years and that I could still clearly recall. Her description of the town where she lived –

a place I had never been to, though I knew it wasn't far from here – and of its beauty had been particularly tenacious: it had often, as I had said, returned to my mind, to the extent that I had wondered why it did. The reason, I thought, was that this description had a finality to it that I couldn't imagine ever attaining in my own circumstances. She had talked about the placid neighbourhood where she had her home with her husband and children, with its cobbled streets too narrow for cars to pass down, so that nearly everyone travelled by bicycle, and where the tall, slender gabled houses were set back behind railings from the silent waterways on whose banks great trees stood, holding out their heavy arms so that they made plunging green reflections in the stillness below, like mirrored mountains. Through the windows you could hear the sounds of footsteps on the cobbles below and the hiss and whirr of bicycles passing in their shoals and drifts; and most of all you could hear the bells that rang unendingly from the town's many churches, striking not just the hours but the quarter and half hours, so that each segment of time became a seed of silence that then blossomed, filling the air with what almost seemed a kind of self-description. The conversation of these bells, held back and forth across the rooftops, was continued night and day: its cadences of observation and agreement, its passages of debate, its longer narratives – at matins and even-song, for instance, and most of all on Sundays, the repeating summons building and building until it was followed at last by the joyous, deafening exposition – comforted her, she had said, as the sound of her parents' lifelong conversation had comforted her in her childhood, the rise and fall of their voices always there in the next room, discussing and observing and noting each thing that happened, as though they were making an inventory of the whole world. The quality of the town's silence, she had said, was something she only really noticed when she went elsewhere, to places where the air was filled with the drone of traffic and of music blaring out of restaurants and shops and the cacophony from the endless construction sites where buildings were forever being torn down and then put up again. She would come home to a silence that at those times felt so refreshing it was like swimming in cool water, and she would for a period be aware of how the bells, far from disturbing the silence, were in fact defending it.

Her description of her life had struck me, I said to her now, as that of a life lived inside the mechanism of time, and whether or not it was a life everyone would have found desirable it had seemed at the very least to lack a quality that drove other people's lives into extremity, whether of pleasure or of pain.

She lifted her elegant eyebrows, her head tilted to one side.

That quality, I said, could almost be called suspense, and it seemed to me to be generated by the belief that our lives were governed by mystery, when in fact that mystery was merely the extent of our self-deception over the fact of our own mortality. I had often thought of her, I said, in the years since we had last met, and those thoughts had tended to occur when I myself had been driven into extremity by the suspicion that some knowledge was being withheld from me whose revelation would make everything clear. She had talked, I said, about her husband and two sons and about the simple, regulated life they lived, a life that involved little change and hence little waste, and the fact that in certain details her life had mirrored my own while in no way resembling it had often led me to see my situation in the most unflattering light. I had broken that mirror, I said, without knowing whether I had done so as an act of violence or simply by mistake. Suffering had always appeared to me as an opportunity, I said, and I wasn't sure I would ever discover whether this was true and if so why it was, because so far I had failed to understand what it might be an opportunity for. All I knew was that it carried a kind of honour, if you survived it, and left you in a relationship to the truth that seemed closer, but that in fact might have been identical to the truthfulness of staying in one place.

The interviewer sat with her light, bony limbs gracefully crossed and an expression of increasing severity on her face, which was deeply lined and shadowed, particularly beneath the eyes, where the skin almost looked bruised. Her head was bent and drooped on her long thin neck like the head of a dark flower while she listened.

'I admit,' she said finally, 'that I took pleasure in telling you about my life and in making you feel envious of me. I was proud of it. I remember thinking, yes, I've avoided making a mess of things, and it seemed to me that it was through hard work and self-control that I had, rather than luck. But it was important not to look as if I was boasting. It always felt then as if I had a secret,' she said, 'and it would have ruined things if I had let it out. When I used to look at my husband I knew that he had the same secret and I knew that he would never tell it either because it was something we shared, like actors secretly share the knowledge that they're acting, which if they openly admitted it would ruin the scene. Actors need an audience,' she said, 'and so did we, because part of the pleasure was showing our secret without telling it.'

Over the years they had watched their contemporaries fall at one hurdle or another and they had even tried to help in these emergencies, which only increased their feeling of superiority. At around the time she met me, she went on, she had a good friend at home who was going through a terrible divorce and who spent a lot of time at their house getting support and advice. The two families had been close and had spent many evenings and weekends and holidays in one another's company, but now a completely different reality was revealed. Every day this friend would appear with some new story of horror: the husband had arrived with a van and taken all the furniture when she wasn't there, or he had left the children alone all weekend when it was his turn to have them; then that he was forcing her to sell the home where they'd lived all their lives and going around to all their friends saying the most awful things about her and poisoning their minds against her. She would sit at our kitchen table, the interviewer said, pouring out these stories in utter shock and dismay and my husband and I would listen and try to comfort her. But at the same time it gave us a kind of pleasure to watch her, though we would never, ever have admitted it to each other, because the pleasure was part of our unspoken secret.

'The fact was,' the interviewer went on, 'that my husband and I had once envied this woman and the man she was married to, whose life at one time had seemed in numerous ways superior to our own. They were very lively and adventurous people,' she said, 'and they were always setting off with their children on exotic travels, and they also had very good taste, so that their home was full of beautiful, unusual objects, as well as the evidence of their creativity and love of high culture. They painted and played musical instruments and read tremendous numbers of books, and as a family they behaved in ways that always seemed more free-spirited and fun than our own family activities managed to be. It was the only time – when we were with them,' she said – 'that I became dissatisfied with our life and with our characters and our children's characters. I envied them, because they seemed to have more than we had, and I couldn't see what they had done to deserve it.'

In short, she had been jealous of this friend, who nevertheless constantly complained about her lot, about the injustices of motherhood or the indignity of the domestic work involved in bringing up a family. Yet the one thing she never complained about was her husband, and perhaps for this reason the husband became the thing the interviewer envied her for most of all, to the extent that he almost succeeded in making her own husband look inadequate to her. He was bigger and more handsome than her husband, extremely charming and sociable, and he possessed a formidable range of physical and intellectual talents, winning every game he played and always knowing more than anyone else on any subject. In addition he was very domesticated and appeared to be the ideal father, spending all his time gardening and cooking with the children and taking them on camping and sailing trips. Most of all he was sympathetic to his wife's complaining, and was always egging her on to become more and more indignant about the travails and oppressions of womanhood, which he himself did so much to relieve her of.

'My own husband,' she said, 'was physically unconfident and also spent so much time in his law office that he missed out on many of our family routines, and these failures – which were the cause of private feelings of resentment and anger for me – I energetically concealed, boasting instead about his importance and how hard he worked, to the extent that I almost succeeded in denying those feelings to myself. Only when we were with this other couple did the truth threaten to become apparent, and I wondered sometimes whether my husband had ever guessed my thoughts or might even have privately suspected me of being in love with this other man. But if it was love,' the interviewer said, 'then it was of the kind the Bible calls covetousness, and my friend's husband enjoyed nothing more than being coveted. Never have I met a man so dedicated to maintaining appearances,' she said, 'to the extent that I came to see something almost female in him, despite the manliness of his persona. I felt a great kinship with him, and never more than when I was boasting about my husband's slavish dedication to his work and he was likewise taking his wife's part and describing some undignified aspect of her life as a woman. In a way we recognised one another: we liked one another as a way of liking ourselves, although of course nothing was ever said because then the picture we had made of our lives would have been completely ruined. My friend once told me,' she went on, 'that her mother had said to her that she didn't deserve her husband. And at the time,' the interviewer said, 'I privately agreed, but in the divorce those words took on an entirely opposite meaning.'

With each fresh story she heard at the kitchen table, she said, she was forced to wonder more and more about the character of this man, which she had at one time found so appealing and even now, with the evidence before her, had trouble condemning. And she would look at her own husband sitting patiently and kindly while their friend talked, even though he was exhausted from work and hadn't even had time to change out of his suit, and she would feel astonished anew at her good sense in choosing him. The more terrible things their friend said about the other man, the more she hoped no one had noticed how much she had liked him, to the extent that she began to criticise him harshly, even though she still secretly thought the friend might be exaggerating the things he had done. And her husband, she noticed, was unusually critical of him too, so that she began to see that he had actually hated him all along.

'It started to seem,' she said, 'as if between us we had somehow brought about the destruction of their family life, as if my secret love and his secret hate had conspired to destroy the object of their disagreement. Each night after our friend had gone home we would sit and talk quietly about her situation, and it felt like we were writing a story together,' she said, 'where things that never happened in reality were allowed to happen and justice could be done, and it all seemed to be coming from inside our own heads, except that it was also happening in actuality. We became closer than we had been in a while. It was a good time in our marriage,' she said, with a bitter smile. 'It was as if all the things we had envied in that other marriage had been released and bequeathed to us.'

She turned her head, still smiling, and looked down the hill towards the city, where cars were moving in swarms along the roads beside the river. The distinctive shape of her nose, which from the front slightly marred her fine-featured face, in profile attained beauty: it was upturned and snub-ended and had a deep V in its bridge, as though someone had drawn it with a certain licence, to make a point about the relationship between destiny and form.

I said that while her story suggested that human lives could be governed by the laws of narrative, and all the notions of retribution and justice that narrative lays claim to, it was in fact merely her interpretation of events that created that illusion. The couple's divorce, in other words, had nothing to do with her secret envy of them and her desire for their downfall: it was her own capacity for storytelling – which, as I had already told her, had affected me all those years ago – that made her see her own hand in what happened around her. Yet the suspicion that her own desires were shaping the lives of other people, and even causing them to suffer, did not seem to lead her to feel guilt. It was an interesting idea, I said, that the narrative impulse might spring from the desire to avoid guilt, rather than from the need – as was generally assumed – to connect things together in a meaningful way; that it was a strategy calculated, in other words, to disburden ourselves of responsibility.

'But you believed my story all those years ago,' she said, 'despite the fact that I didn't expect you to and that probably I only wanted to make my life seem enviable so that I could accept it myself. My whole career,' she said, 'has involved interviewing women – politicians, feminists, artists – who have made their female experience public and who are willing to be honest about one aspect or another of it. It has been up to me to represent their honesty,' she said, 'while at the same time being far too timid to live life in the way they do, according to feminist ideals and political principles. It was easier to think,' she said, 'that my own way of life involved its own courage, the courage of consistency. And I did come to revel in the difficulties such women experienced, while at the same time appearing to sympathise with them.

'As a child,' she said, 'I used to see my sister, who was two years older than me, take the brunt of whatever came, while I watched it all from the safety of my mother's lap, and every time she went wrong or made a mistake, I made a note to myself not to do the same thing when it was my turn. There were often terrible arguments,' she said, 'between my sister and my parents, and I profited from them simply by not being the cause of them, so that when it came to these interviews I found I was in a familiar position. I seemed to profit,' she said, 'from the mere fact of not being these public women, while they were in a sense fighting my cause, just as my sister had fought my cause by demanding certain freedoms that I was then easily granted when I reached the same age. I wondered whether one day I might have to pay for this privilege, and if so whether the reckoning might come in the form of female children, and each time I was pregnant I hoped so ardently for a boy that it seemed impossible that my wish would be granted. Yet each time it was,' she said, 'and I watched my sister struggle with her daughters as I had always watched her struggle with everything, with the satisfaction of knowing that by watching closely enough I had avoided her mistakes. Perhaps for that reason,' she said, 'it was almost unbearable to me when my sister made a success of something. Despite the fact that I loved her, I couldn't tolerate the spectacle of her triumph.

'The friend that I told you about earlier,' she said, 'was in fact my sister, and it did seem to me that her divorce and the destruction of her family was the thing I had been waiting for all my life. In the years that followed,' she said, 'I would sometimes look at her daughters and I would almost hate them for the damage and suffering that showed in their faces, because the sight of these damaged children reminded me that it was not, after all, a game any more, the old simple game where I profited by watching – as it were – from the safety of my mother's lap. My own sons continued to live normal lives full of security and routine, while my sister's house was racked by the most terrible troubles, troubles she continued to be honest about, to the point where I told her I thought she was damaging the children even more by not putting up a pretence for them. In the end I became reluctant to expose my own children to it, because I worried they would find the sight of such violent emotion disturbing, and so I stopped inviting them to our house and to come on holiday with us, as I had regularly done up until then.

'It was at that point,' she said, 'when I took my eyes off my sister's household, that things began to change for her. I noticed, in the communications I still had with my sister, that she sounded calmer and more optimistic; I began to hear stories of her daughters' small successes and improvements. One day,' she said, 'I was on my bicycle and it began suddenly to pour with rain. For once I had come out without my waterproof, and looking for somewhere to shelter, I realised I was close to my sister's house. It was early in the morning and I knew she would be at home, so I pedalled through the rain to her front door and I rang the bell. I was completely bedraggled and soaking wet, as well as wearing my oldest clothes, and it didn't even occur to me that someone other than my sister might open the door. To my surprise, it was a man who opened it, a good-looking man who immediately stepped back to let me in and who took my wet things and offered me a towel to dry my hair with. I knew,' she said, 'the instant I laid eyes on him, that this was my sister's new partner, and that he was a far better man than the husband I had once envied her, and it was indeed the case that he represented a change in her fortunes and in her daughters' fortunes too. I realised,' she said, 'that she was happy for the first time in her life, and I realised too that she would never have known this happiness had she not gone through the unhappiness that preceded it, in precisely the way that she did. She had once said that her former husband's cold and selfish character, which none of us – she least of all – had really perceived, had been like a kind of cancer: invisible, it had lain within her life for years, making her more and more uncomfortable without her knowing what it was, until she had been driven by pain to open everything up and tear it out. It was then that our mother's cruel words – that my sister hadn't deserved her husband – came back to me with their altered meaning. At the time it had seemed inexplicable to us all that my sister would leave such a husband, driving him into acts of whose callousness she was clearly the catalyst and doing irreparable harm to her children, but she now told a different story: his incipient callousness was the thing from which she felt duty-bound to save her children, despite the fact that at the time she couldn't really prove that it was there. My sister told me,' she said, 'that she and her husband were once having a discussion about the former GDR and the awful ways in which people betrayed one another under the regime of the Stasi, and she had made the point that none of us truly knows the extent of our own courage or cowardice, because in these times those qualities are rarely tested. He had disagreed, very strangely: he said that under those same circumstances he knew he would be among the first to sell out his neighbour. That, my sister said, was the first clear glimpse she had had of the stranger inside the man she lived with, though there were many other incidents, obviously, during the course of their marriage that might have told her who he really was, had he not succeeded in persuading her that she had either dreamt them or made them up.

'My sister's daughters now went from strength to strength, and in the public exams they far outshone my own children, who nonetheless did well enough. My sons were pleasant and stable; they had identified career paths for themselves – one in engineering, the other in computer software – and as they prepared to leave school and go out into the world I felt confident they would make responsible citizens. My husband and I, in other words, had done our duty, and it was now that I considered taking some of those feminist principles I had distributed far and wide and using them for myself. The truth was that I had long wondered what might lie outside the circumscribed world of my marriage, and what freedoms and pleasures might be waiting for me there: it seemed to me that I had behaved honourably towards my family and my community, and that this was a moment in which I could, as it were, resign without causing anger or hurt and get away under cover of darkness. And a part of me believed that I was owed this reward for those years of self-control and self-sacrifice, but another part merely wanted to win the game once and for all; to show a woman like my sister that it was possible to gain freedom and self-knowledge without having to smash up the whole world in public in the process.

'I imagined travelling,' she said, 'to India and Thailand, alone with a simple knapsack, moving lightly and swiftly after all the years of being weighed down; I imagined sunsets and rivers, and mountaintops visible on calm evenings. I imagined my husband at home in our house beside the canal, with our sons and his hobbies and his friends, and it seemed to me he might also be relieved,' she said, 'because over the two decades of our marriage our male and female qualities had become blunted on one another. We lived together like sheep, grazing side by side, huddled next to one another in sleep, habituated and unthinking. I considered that there might be other men,' she said, 'and indeed for a long time other men had been appearing in my dreams, which otherwise were full of familiar people and familiar situations and anxieties. But these men who appeared were always strangers, based on no one I had ever known or met, and yet they recognised me with a special tenderness and desire, and I would recognise them too, recognise in their faces something I felt I had once known but had forgotten or never found, and which I only remembered now, in the dream-state. Of course I could never tell anyone about these dreams, from which I woke feeling the most unbearable, exquisite happiness that quickly grew cold in the dawn light of our room and became disappointment. I have always been impatient with people who talk about their dreams,' she said, 'but I had a powerful desire to tell someone about these dreams of mine. Yet the only person I could think of to tell,' she said, 'was the man in the dream himself.

'At around this time,' she went on, 'my husband began to change, in ways that were so small they were impossible to identify and at the same time impossible to ignore. It was almost as if he had become a copy or forgery of himself, someone otherwise identical who nonetheless lacked the authentic quality of the original. And indeed whenever I asked him what was wrong, he would always say the same thing, which was that he wasn't feeling quite himself. I asked our sons if they had noticed anything and for a long time they denied it, but one evening, after the three of them had gone together to a football match – something they did regularly – they admitted that I was right and that he was somehow different. Again, it was impossible to say what the difference was, since he looked and behaved as normal. But he wasn't really there, they said, and it occurred to me that this quality of absence might signify that he was having an affair. And indeed one evening in the kitchen shortly afterwards he suddenly said, very sombrely, that he had some news for me. In that moment,' she said, 'I felt our whole life cleave apart, as though someone had cut it open with a great bright blade; I almost felt I could see the sky and the open air through the ceiling of our kitchen and feel the wind and rain coming through the walls. I had watched other couples separate,' she said, 'and it was usually like the separation of Siamese twins, a long-drawn-out agony that in the end makes two incomplete and sorrowing people out of what was one. But this was so swift and sudden,' she said, 'a mere slicing of the rope that tethered us, that it felt almost painless. My husband was not having an affair, however,' she said, tilting her head back towards the dull grey sky and blinking her eyes several times. 'What he had to tell me was not that our life together was over and that I was free, but that he was ill,' she said, 'an illness, moreover, that would not hasten his death but would instead blight every aspect of the life that remained to him. We had been married for twenty years,' she said, 'and he could easily live twenty more, the doctors had told him, each day losing some facet of his autonomy and potency, a reverse kind of evolution that would require him to pay back every single thing he had taken from life. And I too would have to pay,' she said, 'because the one thing that was forbidden to me was to desert him in his time of need, despite the fact that I no longer loved him and perhaps had never really loved him, and that equally he might not have ever loved me either. This would be the last secret we had to keep,' she said, 'and the most important one, because if this secret got out all the others would too, and the whole picture of life and of our children's lives we had made would be destroyed.

'My sister's new partner,' she went on after a while, 'has a house on one of the islands, the most beautiful island of them all. My husband and I had often fantasised about owning a property there, despite the fact that we could not have afforded even the smallest cowshed in that place. But it would have made our family complete, we felt, and it was something we always wanted that nonetheless remained outside our grasp. I have seen photographs of her partner's house,' she said, 'which is a spectacular place right by the water, and her children are sometimes in the photographs, and even though I know them well they look like happy strangers. But I have never been to that house,' she said, 'and I will never go, despite the fact that my sister increasingly spends all her time there and even manages to complain about certain aspects of it, so that I have wondered whether one day she will reject it, as she has rejected nearly everything else she's been given. I no longer know what goes on inside my sister's head,' she said, 'because she no longer tells me, and it is this fact – that her life now has a secret of its own – that proves to me she will, after all, hold on to what she has. I sense that she would like never to see me again, and perhaps even never to see anyone. She has come to the end of her journey, a journey I have spent my whole life watching her make, and she has found what she wanted, despite my watching her with the greatest ambivalence. The effect has been to make her disappear from my view, as though I have forfeited my right to be able to see her. And I can't get over the feeling,' she said, 'that all of it was stolen from me.'

She was silent for a while, her chin lifted and her eyes half-closed. A bird landed enquiringly at her feet on the gravel path and sprang away again unnoticed.

'Now and again,' she continued presently, 'I have met people who have freed themselves from their family relationships. Yet there often seems to be a kind of emptiness in that freedom, as though in order to dispense with their relatives they have had to dispense with a part of themselves. Like the man trapped in the glacier who cut off his own arm,' she said, with a faint smile. 'I don't intend to do that. My arm occasionally hurts me but I see it as my duty to keep it. The other day,' she said, 'I met her first husband in the street. He was walking along holding a briefcase and wearing a suit, and I was surprised because this businessman's attire was something I had never associated with him: he had always been a bohemian, artistic kind of person, and the fact that he would never stoop to working in an office – even if it meant his family were hard up – and condescended to the people who did, was one of the things that I guessed had riled my husband about him. My sister had earned the money in their household, and had even claimed – as a matter of feminist principle – to be glad that she did, but after their divorce I suppose he had eventually had to fend for himself. In fact I had privately admired his contempt for conventional men, and indeed I secretly shared it, so it was a surprise to me, as I say, to see him apparently dressed as one. We approached each other in the street and our eyes met, and I felt my old fondness for him spring up, in spite of everything that had happened. When we drew close enough I opened my mouth to speak, and only then did I see the expression of utter hatred on his face, so that for a moment I thought he might actually be about to spit at me. Instead, as he passed me, he hissed. It was a sound,' she said, 'such as an animal would make, and I was so shocked that I simply stood there in the street for a long time after he had walked away. The bells began to ring,' she said, 'and at the same time it started to rain, and I stood with my eyes fixed on the pavement, where the water was beginning to gather and to show the buildings and the trees and the people upside down in reflection. The bells rang and rang,' she said, 'and it must have been some special occasion, because I didn't think I had ever heard them ring for so long, to the point where I believed they would never stop. The melody they played got wilder and wilder and more and more nonsensical. But for as long as they rang,' she said, 'I was unable to move, and so I stood there with the water running down my hair and over my face and my clothes, watching the whole world gradually transfer itself into the mirror at my feet.'

She fell silent, her mouth stretched in a strange grimace, her huge eyes unblinking and the declivity of her nose a well of shadow in the changing light of the garden.

'You asked me earlier,' she said to me, 'whether I believed that justice was merely a personal illusion.

I don't have the answer to that,' she said, 'but I know that it is to be feared, feared in every part of you, even as it fells your enemies and crowns you the winner.'

Then, without saying anything more, she began to put her things in her bag with light, quick movements and turned to me with her hand outstretched. I took it, and felt the surprising smoothness and warmth of her skin.

'I think I have everything I need,' she said. 'In fact I looked up all the details before I came. It's what we journalists do nowadays,' she said. 'One day they'll probably replace us with a computer program. I read that you got married again,' she added. 'I admit that it surprised me. But don't worry,' she said, 'I won't be focusing on the personal elements. What matters is that it's a long, important piece. If I can get it done by the morning,' she said, looking at her watch, 'they may even put it in the afternoon edition.'

The party was being held at a venue in the city centre and a guide had been appointed to accompany those who wished to walk there from the hotel. He was a tall, thin boy with thick, lustrous black hair that grew in waves nearly down to his shoulders and a fixed brilliant smile that he displayed continuously while his eyes moved rapidly from side to side, as though he had learned to remain alert to the possibility of ambush.

He often guided participants around the city, he told me, since his mother was the festival's director and had decided in this way to make use of his navigational abilities, which he had been told were unusual. His recollection of pretty much every place he'd been in his life was entirely clear, as well as that of many places he hadn't been, since he liked to study maps in his spare time and to set himself topographical challenges that were often very satisfying to resolve. He had never visited Berlin, for instance, but he was fairly sure that if he were dropped in the middle of it he'd be able to find his way around and might even outwit some of the natives in getting, say, from the swimming pool in Plötzensee to the Berlin public library in the shortest possible time. He had worked out that by emerging from the U-Bahn at Hauptbahnhof and cutting across the Tiergarten on foot, you could save yourself a complicated set of interchanges by train as well as ten or fifteen minutes of time. It had worried him that this shortcut would be less feasible in winter, when he understood the weather in Berlin could be extraordinarily severe, but then the happy thought had occurred to him that since the swimming pool was open-air, you would be unlikely to need to visit it outside the summer months.

We had left the grounds of the hotel by now and were walking down a tunnel-like road with high concrete walls to either side where the steady roar of traffic from the overpass was so loud that Hermann, as he had introduced himself, put his fingers in his ears before darting suddenly down a narrow alleyway to the left. The problem with taking a group for a walk, he went on while we waited for the others to follow, lay in working out how to reach the end all at the same time while accommodating different styles and rates of progress. The faster walkers had to stop frequently to let the slower ones catch up: this meant that the fittest members of the group were given the most opportunity to rest, while those who struggled to keep up were never allowed a chance to catch their breath. Yet if the slowest were given as many stops as the fastest, the walk would have taken approximately double the time: in addition, the fastest would now be waiting twice as long as before, which created new problems such as boredom and frustration, or becoming hungry or cold. His mother had reassured him that these were problems to which he was capable of finding logical solutions, but he was aware that many of what appeared to him as rational challenges appeared to other people as metaphors, and he was always anxious lest a misunderstanding should arise. All his life his mother had encouraged him to read books, not because she was one of those people who believed reading books improved people but because she had pointed out that studying imaginative works would at least enable him to follow certain conversations and not mistake them for reality. As a child he had found stories very upsetting, and he still disliked being lied to, but he had come to understand that other people enjoyed exaggeration and make-believe to the extent that they regularly confused them with the truth. He had learned to absent himself mentally in such situations, he added, by going over passages he had memorised from philosophical texts and revisiting certain maths problems, or sometimes by just reciting some of the more obscure bus timetables in his repertory, until the moment passed.

The others had by now turned the corner into the alley and Hermann set off again, walking rapidly until we emerged into a public park, where he stopped on a path to wait once more. This park was a very pleasant place, he said, though it had a bad reputation, because its crime rate was higher than that of other parks in the city. It also represented a very convenient shortcut by bicycle from his home on the other side of the river to his college, to the extent that it would have taken him fully ten minutes longer to make the same journey along the roads. It astonished him that his classmates, many of whom had to do the same or similar journeys, had not performed the simple calculation that revealed a greater risk of injury from the road than from the park, and continued to take the more hazardous option. Their parents, they admitted, insisted on it, and his mother had explained this anomaly to him by saying that the biological basis of parenthood was essentially antithetical to reason, and as such could be seen as a whole system of inverted logic. She was generally speaking a logical person, he said, and although she admitted the near-impossibility of bringing up a child without sentiment coming into it, he recognised that she had done her best to attain that goal, in this case continuing to support his choice of route even after the college head himself had approached her with concerns for his safety.

The park was a long, sloping stretch of green that descended to the riverbank, with wide sandy paths where people walked or sat on benches in the dusk. In the distance, a group of men wearing high-visibility jackets could be seen standing in a circle on the grass, and Hermann explained that these men were employed to prevent people crossing that particular section of the park. In the attempt to regenerate the area, he said, a new concert hall had not long ago been built that represented a triumph for compromise, in that it satisfied both the city planners' ambitions for progress and the conservationists' determination to keep things as they were. Instead of destroying the park to make way for the new building, the architect had devised a brilliant scheme for constructing the auditorium underground. It was only when the work had been done and the life of the park was permitted to return to normal – without a single thing, superficially, having changed – that it became apparent the acoustics of the concert hall were caused to function in reverse by the traffic overhead. Instead of magnifying the music, the sound of even a single person walking across the grass was intensified in the hall below to quite deafening proportions.

Since the whole thing had been designed to be unnoticeable and for the appearance of the park to be unaffected it was seen as absurd to put up a barrier or fence around an apparently empty stretch of grass, and for the same reasons – because they couldn't see the change – people continued to traverse the grass as they always had. The solution the planners found to this problem, he said, was to employ these men to act as a human fence when there was a concert underway. What they failed to recognise, he went on, his brilliant smile intensifying, was that a fence or sign has a meaning that is clear to almost everybody, whereas a human individual – even one wearing a high-visibility jacket – has to explain himself. When at certain times of day someone approached the section of grass, he said, which the rest of the time they were permitted to cross freely, one of the men would have to explain why they couldn't, and this elaborate procedure, Hermann said, had to be repeated over and over again each day, until inevitably issues of aggression and enforcement arose, since no actual law existed to prevent people crossing the grass and even the fact of a concert being underway didn't strike some as sufficient justification to change their route. Meanwhile, the people attending the concert were becoming infuriated by the noise and asking for their money back. I believe, he said, that some of the incidents that ensued have actually gone to court, and since the purpose of the law is to determine objectivity, it will be interesting to see the outcomes of those cases. He liked to study knotty legal points in his spare time, he added, some of which were actually quite entertaining. His personal favourite was a case in which a woman was driving her car through town when an entire swarm of bees flew in through the window, which she had left open a couple of inches because it was a very hot day. In the ensuing panic she drove the car into the shop-front of a nearby patisserie, causing a great deal of damage – though luckily no loss of human life – for which both she and her insurers believed she was not responsible, a belief in which they were thoroughly confounded by the judge.

I asked Hermann what kind of college he went to and he said it was a specialised school for maths and the sciences that took students from all over the country. Before that he had gone to his neighbourhood school, he said, which he hadn't enjoyed quite so much, though towards the end of his time there he had in fact become quite popular with the other pupils, once it became known he was able to help them with revision for the public exams. He hadn't got on all that well with his teachers, however, and had often had to hear his mother be criticised on his account, for which he was very sorry, but since she herself had never criticised him he had proceeded on the assumption that all was well. It was human nature, his mother said, for people to wish cruelty on one another simply because they had been shown cruelty themselves: the repetition of behavioural forms was the curious panacea with which most people sought to relieve the suffering caused by precisely those same forms. He had tried to find a way of expressing this contradiction in mathematical terms, but since it was inherently illogical he had not yet succeeded. As far as he knew a problem couldn't be solved simply by infinitely restating it, unless you relied on infinity itself to break certain factors down.

The others were now drawing close to us along the path and Hermann set off again downhill across the grass towards the river, pointing exaggeratedly with his hand raised above his head to signal our direction.

He apologised, he said, if I found him too talkative: he liked talking, and had always been encouraged by his mother to ask questions, so it had surprised him to discover that other people rarely asked each other anything. He had come to the conclusion that most questions were nothing more than an attempt to ascertain conformity, like rudimentary maths problems. Two and two did indeed usually equal four: it was when you gave a different answer, he had discovered, that people got upset. According to his mother he had been completely silent until the age of three: she had got into the habit of talking to herself aloud with no expectation of a reply, and she was therefore very surprised when one day as she was looking for her keys and asking herself where she'd put them, he informed her from his highchair that the keys were in the pocket of her coat, which was hanging in the hall. After that he had talked non-stop, and if his mother found it irritating she had always been too polite to say so. Interestingly, he had recently made a friend at college who mispronounced nearly every word he used, because although his vocabulary was impressive, he had read far more than he had spoken, and in complex conversations such as those he had with Hermann, he was uttering words aloud that until now had remained as mere meaningful letter sequences in his head. Hermann was lucky that he had been able to talk so much with his mother, who understood most of what he said: he realised that for many parents and children, this wasn't always the case.

Part of what he enjoyed about college, he said, was that for the first time he was meeting people whose experiences resembled his own and who thought about the world in much the same way he did. It was funny to think that all along, while he'd been sitting at home looking out of his bedroom window, these other people in other places had been looking out of theirs, all of them thinking about similar things, things no one else appeared to think about. He wasn't, in other words, in a minority any more; in fact, he had even discovered that a few of his classmates had a superior grasp in some areas, for instance his friend Jenka, with whom he spent a great deal of his time. He and Jenka got on extremely well, and their mothers had become good friends too. The two women had recently gone on a walking holiday together in the Pyrenees, which was the first holiday his mother had ever taken without him, so he hoped she hadn't missed him too much. He and Jenka were quite different, he added, which interestingly seemed to be the reason they were friends. For instance, Jenka seldom spoke, while he found it difficult to shut up: that was an example of compatibility, in that two extremes were modified by being combined. It was said by certain people at college that Jenka was possibly the most intelligent person of her age in the country. She never said anything unless she had something important to express, which made you realise how much of what people generally said – and he included himself in this statement – was unimportant.

At the end of the year, he went on, the college gave a special award to its most outstanding male and female student. It was interesting that in conferring this award, the fact of gender was retained beyond that of excellence: at first it had struck him as illogical, but then he had decided that having never personally found gender to be a factor, he was perhaps not in a position to fully understand its significance. He would be interested to hear my opinion on that subject, if I had one. His mother, for instance, believed that male and female were distinct but equal identities, and that having two awards was as far as it was wise to go in honouring human achievement. But many other people felt that there should be only one award, given to the best student. The caveat of gender, these people believed, obscured the triumph of excellence. His mother's response to that was interesting: if there was no caveat, she had said, then there was no way of ensuring that excellence would remain in a moral framework and not be put in the service of evil. He had found that argument a little old-fashioned, which was surprising since his mother was usually quite forward-thinking. Her use of the word 'evil' in particular had been quite a shock. He wondered sometimes what her life was going to be like, once he left next year to go to university, but though he did appear to possess certain talents, unfortunately a good imagination wasn't one of them.

We were now walking directly beside the river, on a wider paved path where people sat outside cafés with large, luminous glasses of beer in front of them, talking or looking at their phones or staring absently at the greyish water. It wasn't much further to our destination, Hermann said, but this was the riskiest part of the journey since it was more crowded here, and the possibility of things going wrong tended to be proportionate to the size of the human element. Also, he was finding our conversation very interesting, so there was the additional danger of forgetting where he was supposed to be going. But he did wish to hear my opinion of the topics discussed, and most particularly of his mother's remarks, that is if he had managed to relay them correctly.

I said I had been struck by the idea of gender as a bulwark against evil, because the biblical myth gave one precisely the opposite impression: that, far from preventing evil, the mutual distinctness of male and female constitutes a unique susceptibility to it. Eve is influenced by the serpent and Adam is influenced by Eve: I didn't know very much about maths, I said, but I would be interested to know whether that could be expressed as a formula, and if so whether the serpent would be an illogical element of it. In other words, I imagined it would be hard to ascribe a value to the serpent, which could be anything and everything. All the story proves, I said, is that Adam and Eve are equally capable of being influenced, but by different things.

Hermann furrowed his brow and said that it might be easier to see it as a shape: expressed as a triangle, for instance, the Adam/Eve/serpent relationship is more tangible, since the function of triangulation is to fix two points by means of a third and therefore establish objectivity. If I was interested in metaphors, he said, the serpent's role is merely to create a viewpoint from which Adam's and Eve's weaknesses can be observed, and thus the snake might be representative of anything that triangulates the relationship of two identities, such as the arrival of a child might triangulate its parents. He went on to say that as far as this last point was concerned, his own case was more complicated, since through force of circumstances he had played Adam, as it were, to his mother's Eve. He had never met his father, his having left the planet a few weeks before Hermann arrived on it: he had been worrying that he had failed to include this piece of information in our conversation so far and was glad I had given him the opportunity to fit it in. As it happened he had often wondered whether he and his mother would be triangulated, and if so by whom. Unfortunately the only available role was that of serpent, he added, and he admitted that he had kept an eye open for the arrival of that disturbing presence. But to date his mother had not remarried, though she was very beautiful – that was merely an opinion, by the way – and when he had asked her what the probability was that she ever would, she had replied that such a step would require her to become two people, and that she would prefer just to remain one. His mother rarely spoke figuratively, because she knew it upset him, but he accepted that on this occasion she had decided on it as the lesser of two – if I would permit him to use the word again – evils. He believed she meant that her biological role as his mother would be incompatible with the role of wife to someone biologically unrelated, and this realisation had made him feel guilty, to the extent that he thought the best thing would be for him to leave the house immediately and find some means of destroying himself. But happily she had offered a clarification, which was that she was happy with things as they were.

To return to the subject of the college's award, he said, the name they had chosen for it was 'Kudos'. As

I was probably aware, the Greek word 'kudos' was a singular noun that had become plural by a process of back formation: a kudo on its own had never actually existed, but in modern usage its collective meaning had been altered by the confusing presence of a plural suffix, so that 'kudos' therefore meant, literally, 'prizes', but in its original form it connoted the broader concept of recognition or acclaim, as well as being suggestive of something which might be falsely claimed by someone else. For instance, he had heard his mother complaining to someone on the phone the other day that the board of directors took the kudos for the festival's success while she did all the work. In light of his mother's remarks about male and female, the choice of this fabricated plural was quite interesting: the individual had been superseded by the collective, yet he believed that it still left the question of evil entirely open. Admittedly, despite extensive research, he had been unable to find anything to corroborate his mother's use of the word in a context of misappropriation. Could prizes be given to the wrong person, without malintent coming into it?

He hadn't asked the college whether his award – perhaps he had forgotten to mention that he had won it, alongside his friend Jenka – was a kudo or a kudos, but he supposed the college wasn't overly concerned with the grammatical perspective. It had been very pleasant to win: his mother had been extremely happy, though he had had to ask her not to become unnecessarily emotional.

The others were dawdling along the waterfront and we stopped to wait for them to catch up. My phone rang and my older son's number appeared on the screen.

'Guess what I'm doing right now,' he said.

Tell me, I said.

'Walking out through the school gates for the very last time,' he said.

Congratulations, I said.

I asked him how the final exam had gone.

'Surprisingly well,' he said. 'In fact, I actually enjoyed it.'

I might remember, he said, that he had spent a lot of time revising a subject – the history of representations of the Madonna – that had never once come up in any of the past papers he had looked at. He had worked and worked at it, all the time doubting the rationale for these labours but unable to convince himself to stop. Opening the exam paper, the very first question had concerned that subject.

'I had so much to say,' he said, 'that I forgot I was in an exam. It was actually a pleasure. I couldn't quite believe it.'

He should believe it, I said, since it had a concrete explanation, which was that he had worked hard.

'I suppose so,' he said. There was a silence. 'When are you coming home?' he said.

When we had finished speaking Hermann asked me if my child or children were good at maths. I said that neither of them had pursued that subject, which I sometimes worried was the consequence of my own interests lying in a different direction, so that I had involuntarily made some aspects of the world seem realer and more important to them than others. Hermann smiled delightedly at the impossibility of this idea: there was no reason, he said, to trouble myself on that account, since research had proved that parental influence over personality outcomes was virtually nil. A parent's effect lay almost entirely in the quality of his or her nurture and of the home environment, much as a plant will wilt or thrive according to where it is placed and how it is cared for, while its organic structure remains inviolable. His mother, for instance, recollected that she had ceased to be able to answer his questions without recourse to textbooks somewhere between the ages of four and five. His interest in maths, in other words, pre-existed any attempt to encourage or thwart him; unless I had gone out of my way to prevent my children from showing such an interest then it was unlikely that I had played any role.

I said that on the contrary I had known many people whose ambitions were the result of parental influence, and many others who had been prevented from becoming what they had wanted to be. The children of artists had been – in my experience – particularly susceptible to their parents' values, as if one person's freedom became the next person's yoke. I found this idea peculiarly repugnant, I said, because it hinted at something beyond mere neglect or selfishness, a special kind of egotism that sought to eliminate the risks of creativity by enslaving others to its point of view. And there were other people who had acquired what we might regard as a God-given talent through sheer force of will. I didn't, in other words, accept the primacy of preordination: to return to his remarks about plants, what that analogy left out was the human possibility of self-creation.

Hermann was silent for a while, and standing beside the bridge we watched the broken shapes its reflection made in the water. He believed that Nietzsche, he said presently, had taken for his motto a phrase of Pindar's: become what you are. Perhaps, in other words, we could agree to disagree, as long as that phrase meant the same thing to both of us. If he understood me correctly, I ascribed to outside factors the capacity to alter the self, while at the same time believing the self capable of determining or even altering its own nature. He recognised that he had been very fortunate in that no one, as yet, had tried to stop him being what he was; I myself had perhaps not been so lucky. But the phrase was interesting insofar as it posited the fact of self as a truth, in a manner that made cogito ergo sum look frankly banal. An initial response might be to ask how something can become what it already is: he believed we had established some parameters for quite an interesting conversation on that subject. Perhaps if I found myself with some spare time over the next couple of days, we could continue it.

The rest of the group were drawing close and Hermann fell silent, counting them. The same number of people had arrived, he remarked, as had set out: he supposed he should consider the possibility, since he hadn't been paying them much attention, that one or more members of the group had been removed and replaced by others along the way, but all in all it was pretty unlikely. The venue was just on the other side of this bridge, he said: if I looked, I could see it from here. He hoped I hadn't found his company annoying, he added. He realised that he wasn't always able to tell whether his presence was wanted or not. But as far as he was concerned, it had been a very pleasant walk.

There was a long queue for food at the bar, where the waiters were having trouble operating the coupon system. The room was a cavernous modern space with a high cantilevered glass ceiling, which had the effect of intensifying the din of music and conversation while at the same time making the people in the room appear dwarfed and small, so that the occasion seemed gripped by an atmosphere of panic to which the presence of so many reflecting surfaces only added. It was dark by now, and electric light rained down in crossing lance-shapes through the glass ceiling from the buildings out-side while the black body of the river undulated just beyond the windows, with the human figures inside interposed in reflection on its churning surfaces.

The problem, the woman next to me observed, was that the coupons came in denominations that didn't match the prices of the food, and so the question of how to give change had not been resolved. Also, some people wanted to eat and drink more than others, yet we had all been given the same amount. She her-self ate little, being small and also of a certain age; a grown man with an appetite would need three times as much. She could see, however, that as far as the festival was concerned, it would have been imprac-ticable to have given their guests free rein with an infinite number of coupons, and also unfair to have discriminated between them on the basis of need, for who can ever say what another's needs are? And at this point, she said, looking resignedly at the queue, at the head of which a number of waiters were lengthily conferring and studying the coupons in puzzlement while the people queuing were showing signs of increasing unrest, we're unlikely to get anything at all. We invent these systems with the aim of ensuring fairness, she said, and yet the human situation is so complex that it always evades our attempts to encompass it. While we are fighting the war on one front, she said, on another chaos has arisen, and there are many regimes that have come to the conclusion it is human individuality that causes all the problems. If people were all the same, she said, and shared a single point of view, it would of course make us much easier to organise. And that, she said, is where the real problems start.

She was a tiny, sinewy woman with a childlike body and a large, bony, sagacious face in which the big, heavy-lidded eyes had an almost reptilian patience, occasionally slowly blinking. She had attended my event this afternoon, she added, and had been struck as she often was by the inferiority of these occasions to the work that was their subject, which seemed to be circled with increasing aimlessness and never penetrated. We get to walk in the grounds, she said, but we never enter the building. The purpose of festivals like this one had become less and less clear to her, despite the fact that she was on its board of directors, while the personal value of books had – for her at least – increased; yet she had the sense that the attempt to make a public concern out of a private pastime – reading and writing – was spawning a literature of its own, in that many of the writers invited here excelled at public appearances while producing work she found frankly mediocre. In the case of such people, she said, there are only the grounds: the building isn't there, or if it is, it's a temporary structure that will be swept away by the next storm. But she recognised, she said, that her age might have something to do with this jaded perspective. Increasingly she found herself turning away from the contemporary, back towards the landmarks of literary history. Lately she had been rereading Maupassant, and was finding it as fresh and as charming as on the day it had been written. Meanwhile, the unstoppable juggernaut of commercial literary success pressed on, though she had the sense that the marriage between the two principles – commerce and literature – was not in the best of health. A small adjustment in public tastes, she said, a thoughtless decision to spend one's money on something else, and the whole thing – the global enterprise of fiction publishing and its affiliated industries – could be gone in an instant, leaving the small rock of authentic literature where it always was.

She was wearing a tissue-like black shawl and she drew it back to hold out a small bony hand to me with numerous glinting antique rings on the fingers, introducing herself by a name so long and complex I had to ask her to repeat it. Just call me Gerta, she said, waving the question away with a thin-lipped smile: the rest of it was a pointless mouthful. In a few decades' time, she said, no one will care about such names any more, even though to their owners they were a sacred responsibility. She had four children, she said, and none of them cared in the slightest about their birthright or who might inherit what. Just don't leave us in a situation we might argue about, they had said to her recently, and it was true that her own generation had been beset by the most extraordinary rifts and feuds over questions of inheritance. But her children didn't care about money or land, perhaps because they had always had them and had seen how little good they did. Or rather, they had seen enough to know that only the finest of lines separated them from their forebears, and that all she had to do was weight the scales in one direction or another to condemn them to the same fate. They had urged her countless times to sell the family estates and enjoy the profits in her own lifetime, down to the last drop, she said, laughing, as though this feeble body of mine was capable of using up all our assets and turning them to transient pleasures. Her own father, she said, had been extraordinarily parsimonious, in his later years living mostly off dry crackers and small cubes of cheese: he had been known to turn up at grand dinners bearing an opened bottle of supermarket wine from which he had drunk perhaps a single glass a few weeks earlier, when his hosts might have hoped for an offering from his extensive vineyards. It was this asceticism of her father's, she said, which she had always interpreted as a determination not to make a dent in the family fortunes, that stopped her selling or giving away what had been passed on to her. Yet now, she said, I wonder whether it wasn't in fact a kind of vice or an expression of his anger. He had painstakingly rebuilt those fortunes, decimated by two world wars, but it seemed to her that the trauma of early life did more damage than the trauma of history. When he was a child, she said, and the estate was in its heyday, the servants would kneel before his own father to offer him the fruits of the day's hunt or harvest. He had a nanny who killed his white rabbit as a punishment for some misdemeanour or other, and appeared the next day wearing the muff she had fashioned from its skin. It is impossible to recover, she said, from such grandiosity and such cruelty, or from the fatal combination of the two. History goes over the top like a steamroller, she said, crushing everything in its path, whereas childhood kills the roots. And that is the poison, she said, that seeps into the soil.

Yet in her heart she believed that without history there was no identity, and so she couldn't ultimately understand her children's lack of interest in their past, nor their devotion to the cult of happiness. Theirs is a world without war, she said, but it is also a world without memory. They forgive so easily, it is almost as if nothing matters. They are kind to their own children, she said, kinder than our generation ever was, yet their lives seem to me to be without beauty. She paused and slowly blinked her eyes.

Perhaps fifteen years ago, she went on, when the youngest one was leaving home, my husband and I spoke about getting divorced, and though we both wanted to be free, in the end we weren't prepared to put our children through the pain of dismantling the world they knew. It seemed to be enough, that we had both admitted to each other how we felt, and so we have continued to live more or less as we were, she said, except with this admission between us. My husband farms the estate, because this is how he has always made himself feel necessary and useful, and I take care of the administration and other public duties arising from my interest in the arts. We speak to each other very little, she said, and because the house is so big we can sometimes go for days without seeing one another. We have many house guests, she said, because the estate is in a very beautiful part of the countryside, and I have many writer friends who find it an ideal place to work, and perhaps it is the case that I make sure there is other company so that my husband and I are rarely there alone. Our children and our grandchildren come to stay, she said, always with their great mountains of plastic equipment and their special foods and electronic games, and they find us as they have always found us, except that what was once between us is no longer there. And I wonder, she said, whether we haven't done them a great disservice in sparing them this pain, which might somehow have brought them to life, at the same time as knowing that this couldn't possibly be true, and that it is only my own belief in the value of suffering that makes me think it. I am one of those who believes that without suffering there can be no art, she said, and I have no doubt that my love of literature in particular stems from the desire to be confirmed in that belief. Sometimes, she said, when I wake early in the morning I like to go and walk our land, because it reassures me that the decisions I've made are the right ones. Particularly in the mornings of early summer, she said, when the sun is rising through the mist, it has a beauty that can't be put into words. It is still the greatest joy I know, she said, but it has its own cruelty too, because at its most beautiful, she said, it is capable of giving me the illusion that there would have been other, greater joys, had this one not been handed to me as my destiny. She smiled her thin-lipped smile. It may be the case, she said, that it is only when it is too late to escape that we see we were free all along.

She would have to go without nourishment, she added, since the queue had barely moved in all this time: she had to be up early in the morning to take care of her grandchildren, and in any case she no longer had the constitution for staying late at parties.

'I hope we meet again,' she said, withdrawing a small white card from the folds of her shawl and putting it in my hand. 'As I told you, many writers have found my home an ideal place to work, and since there is plenty of space you wouldn't be disturbed. I expect you to take me up on it,' she said, her large unblinking eyes moving slowly around the room. A few feet away from us stood an etiolated man who was leaning on a walking stick, and for a moment I thought it might be Gerta's husband since she looked at him so penetratingly, but then I saw that despite his gaunt appearance and elderly demeanour he was in fact no more than forty-five. He came limping towards us on his stick and greeted Gerta, who kissed him warmly on both cheeks.

'You've caught me creeping away,' Gerta said. 'I'm too old for so many people and so much noise.'

'Ah, nonsense,' he said. He spoke in an Irish accent that had a faintly transatlantic note. 'They just haven't put your favourite music on yet. How're you doing,' he said, to me.

'You know each other, of course,' Gerta said.

It had been some years, Ryan said, but yes, we'd met a few times before.

He crinkled his forehead, apparently in the effort to remember the last occasion. His skin hung so loosely on his face that it formed clown-like folds that accentuated his changes of expression, and the room's harsh light gave it a ghastly, almost ghoulish cast. He was wearing a pale linen suit that similarly hung on him in loose folds, and the electric light dramatised the folds so that he almost looked as if he were wrapped in bandages. He had the appearance of someone who had been hit by extremity, even by some retributive force that had harried him and then left him, chastened and depleted, to limp on, an impression to which his walking stick contributed the final touch. I found myself wondering what he had done to deserve it, and whether I myself was in some way responsible for it, because at one time I had believed that people like Ryan lived their lives with impunity.

'Ryan spoke at the town hall this evening,' Gerta

111

said, raising her voice tremulously above the noise. 'It was a huge success.'

'They were a great crowd,' Ryan said.

'The subject was unity in an era of self-interest,' Gerta said to me. 'It was an interesting panel. Ryan caused quite a stir.'

'All I said,' Ryan said, 'was that I didn't think the two were mutually exclusive.'

'It is a topical issue,' said Gerta, 'since you British are thinking of asking for a divorce.'

'Not guilty,' Ryan said cheerily. 'I'm a happily married Irishman.'

'It will be a great mistake,' Gerta said, 'as perhaps it always is.'

Ryan waved this away with his spare hand, gripping his walking stick with the other.

'It'll never happen,' he said. 'It's like the wife threatening to leave me every Friday night after she's had a few. Not only can the falcon hear the falconer,' he added significantly, 'it's got into the habit of eating out of his hand.'

Gerta laughed.

'Marvellous,' she said.

'The one thing you can say about people for sure,' Ryan said, 'is that they'll only free themselves if freedom is in their own interest.'

'You must come and see us in the countryside,'

Gerta said, reaching into her shawl and giving him one of the white cards she had given me. 'Who knows, you might find the inspiration there to write a follow-up to your phenomenon. I would like to think we had contributed a little bit of the magic.'

'Absolutely,' Ryan said, his narrow eyes moving around the room. 'Great to see you,' he added, clasping Gerta's hand between his.

'I could see you didn't recognise me for a second there,' he said to me, when we had watched her walk slowly away. 'As a matter of fact it happens all the time so don't worry about it. I've got used to the change,' he said, running a hand through his hair, which was longer than I remembered and worn in a looser, combed-back style, 'but I know it's a shock to folk who haven't seen me in a while. I came across some old photos the other day and I could barely recognise myself, so I know how it feels. To be honest, it even still catches me out sometimes. It's not every day you lose half your body weight, is it? The strange thing is,' he said, 'it sometimes feels like that other half is still there. It's just nobody can see it any more.'

A waiter came past with a tray of drinks and Ryan put up his hand in a gesture of refusal.

'I've weaned myself off that stuff, for a start,' he said. 'The old mother's milk. It helps you sleep though, I have to admit. I'm up at all hours these days. It turns out a lot of people are,' he said. 'Thank God for social media. I had no idea how much was going on. It's almost as if I was living in a different century. Now I'm chatting away with people in LA and Tokyo at three in the morning instead of sleeping off my hangover. The wife's delighted,' he said. 'If the kids wake up they don't go near her any more.'

He had turned so that the light fell on him from a slightly different angle. I saw now that what I had interpreted as the signs of misfortune were in fact those of success, and I wondered how these two extremities could be mistaken for one another so easily. His baggy suit was of a fashionably unstructured design and, like the artful disorder of his hair, was clearly expensive. As for his gaunt appearance, it was the result, he said now, of deciding to put away his knife and fork. In fact it was his wife who started him off on the whole regime, he added, though she never imagined he'd go as far with it as he did.

'The thing is,' he said, 'we're obsessives, aren't we? We don't just leave an idea alone – we have to keep going at it until we've dug it up roots and all. I've noticed that a lot of writers don't take care of themselves physically,' he went on, 'and I have to say I think there's a bit of a snob factor there. They worry that if they were caught doing exercise and watching what they ate, people would think less of them as intellectuals. I prefer the Hemingway model,' he said, 'though without the guns and the self-abuse, obviously. But the physical perfectionism – I mean, why not? Why treat your body as if it's just some carrier bag for your brain? And especially with all this publicity we're involved in now – to look at some of them, you'd think they'd never seen the light of day. They might act like it's because they're a bunch of geniuses, but like I say, it's a bit of a snob thing. Personally I get put off if a writer looks like a tramp – I think, why should I trust your view of the world if you can't even take care of yourself? If you were a pilot, I wouldn't get on board – I wouldn't trust you to take me the distance.'

His transformation began a couple of years ago, he said, when his wife gave him a smartwatch for Christmas. It measured your heart rate and pulse and the distances you covered. It had all the hallmarks of a thoughtless offering, something she'd just randomly picked up, but isn't it the case, he said, that it's the random thing that is so often the tool to lever yourself out of your rut?

'Still, I'll be honest,' he said, 'initially I was disappointed. I mean, I wasn't exactly a couch potato – I went to the gym and I more or less ate my five a day and I thought, is there something I'm missing here? Is this one of those things where you start giving each other meaningless presents because you can't be bothered to work out what the other one wants any more? Obviously,' he said, 'I've moved on since then to something much more sophisticated. This one,' he said, pulling back his cuff and holding out his wrist to show me, 'doesn't just tell you what you've done – it tells you what you've still got left to do. At any point in the day,' he said, 'it can give you the consequences of your actions in terms of a future. The other one was basically just a recording device: you had to interpret the data yourself, and the danger there,' he said, 'is that things can get very subjective.'

But like he'd said, it had started him off, and if the wife had got a bit more than she'd bargained for, she'd reckoned without his tendency to take the ball and run with it. It was amazing, he said, to think that most people looked after their cars better than they looked after their bodies, but in fact there was no more mystery to the human organism than to the average engine. It was mostly just maths, and with the numbers now at his disposal he quickly came to an overwhelming realisation: where until now he had believed himself to be driven by want – a force he had managed with varying degrees of success over the years but never mastered – he began to understand that in fact the driving force was need; and of need it was possible to be not merely the master but the victorious champion. People could want an infinite number of things, but what did we really need? Far less than we thought we did – with the right knowledge, that engine could run so cleanly and economically it barely left a trace of itself. For the seeker after advantage, this was priceless information: it represented a whole different sphere of control, in which one could become virtually invisible and therefore invulnerable. To ask oneself the question of what one wanted, on the other hand, was to bog oneself down in the mire, where any and everyone could see you.

'This thing –' he tapped his wrist '– tells me not only what I need but what I've earned, what I could have if I chose to. There's quite a margin there,' he said.

He started to consume only half of what this device told him he had earned and marvelled at the feeling of power it gave him to leave the other half untouched, as though the numbers were actual money in the bank: he was accruing mental capital, as well as running three or four times a week and swimming on his rest days, thereby earning even more. He had wanted to take up cycling too, but at the time he couldn't afford all the fancy equipment, until he realised that the fancy equipment made cycling easier and therefore less profitable, and that he'd do better cycling uphill on his rusty ten-ton three-speed. He didn't know if I'd ever tried running, he said, but it was actually quite meditative: there was a fashion now for writing about it, and if he could find the time he would give the form a go. As for eating, he could take it or leave it these days. Sometimes, watching people eat, it struck him how vulnerable they were; he remembered himself, chomping and chowing through the years, and it seemed to him that by eating he had been trying to make himself safe, when in fact he had been exposing himself. It was as if, by eating, he had hoped to bind himself to the world, to erase the boundary between inside and out. When he thought of all the junk he'd ingested, he wondered how he could have abused himself in that way.

He quickly lost a lot of weight, sure enough, but it was the mental leverage that really made the difference, and with his career going in the way that it had, he thanked God he'd finally seen the light. His book had sat at the top of the *New York Times* bestseller list for six months: I'd doubtless heard of it, though unless I was party to the industry gossip I'd probably never guessed it was anything to do with him, since it was written under a pseudonym. He'd taken on a writing partner, a female ex-student as it happened, and they had made an anagram of their names, though obviously, he said, since he was the front man, as it were, it made sense for their fictional author to be male. At first it had bugged him, he admitted, that success, when it finally turned up, did so under an alias; part of him would have liked to have shown all the doubters back in Tralee. Still, the pseudonym had some of the same advantages as the Nietzschean gimmick on his wrist: it made a part of himself – the part that always seemed fated to the repetition of certain patterns – invisible. There he was sipping wheatgrass juice in first class on a plane to LA, off to meet the people who'd bought the film rights, unrecognisable in every way. The person he'd always been – the Ryan of old – seemed more and more like a childhood friend, someone he was fond of but had left behind, someone of whom he might one day say that he lived in a prison of his own making.

Sara – his writing partner – was happy for him to do the jetting about, since she had her kids to take care of in Galway; and besides, if we were talking about writers letting themselves go, she was a textbook example. She'd once turned up to a meeting with their agent wearing her old slippers, though what she didn't know about fifteenth-century Venice – where the book was set – wasn't worth knowing. The book had originally been her PhD thesis, and as her supervisor he'd found himself giving her all the sterling commercial advice he'd never quite managed to follow himself, so to be able to co-own the project felt like justice at last. It was a sort of marriage, he said, with the books – they were working on another right now – as the offspring. Marriage is still the best model for living, he said, or at least no one's been able to come up with a better one, so why shouldn't it work for writing? And though the offspring were hard work, at least they paid their own way. The wife didn't mind at all – in fact it was she who had suggested it in the first place – and since she'd just bought herself a brand-new Range Rover with the proceeds, he didn't see she was doing too badly out of it either.

I asked him whether he still did any teaching and he grimaced so that the loose skin of his face stood out in eerie folds, before composing his features into an expression of mild regret.

'Much as I'd love to,' he said, 'I just don't have the time any more. Obviously I miss the contact with the students – there's the feeling you're giving something back, isn't there? But to be honest, in the end I started to feel I was selling them a bit of a dud, because there you are encouraging them to think they can write a bestseller and solve all their problems, when actually most of them just don't have the talent. And they take so much from you – to be honest I was desperate to leave, but actually,' he added confidentially, 'they gave me the boot, just before things started to take off. I was on the big dipper there for a while, what with a wife and three kids to support. Obviously,' he said, 'that's not something I'd want put about. But you know,' he said, 'in a way they did me a favour, because I'm not sure I'd have done what I've done if I hadn't been out in the wilderness. You know what it's like,' he said. 'You earn just enough to get by but at the end of the day there's nothing left mentally, and so you cling to the job even harder. The book has changed all that of course,' he said. 'I've been approached by universities in the US – there's some very nice offers on the table, but I'd really have to think about it.'

And life wasn't all roses by any means – it never is. His younger child was diagnosed with autism last year, which was actually a relief, to be able to put a name on it. The wife had the brilliant idea of setting up a charity to help other families with autistic kids, and she'd even got a question asked in the Irish parliament about special needs provision in schools. He'd put together a little anthology to raise money for her, asking writers to contribute stories for free. It was amazing, the response he'd had – there were some very big names in that anthology and all of it was original work, so there'd been a mind-blowing auction for the serial rights.

'Unfortunately,' he said, 'the economics of it meant we couldn't ask people like yourself for contributions, since the whole point of it was to make money and as I say, we needed the big names for that.'

He looked at me with a clown-like expression of

regret, almost of pity. He was glad I was keeping well, he said. It was good to see me here on the circuit – at least I was keeping in the game. He ought to go and circulate, since he was sort of the guest of honour this evening: there were various people expecting to meet him.

He scanned the room with his narrow eyes and then turned back to me, raising his walking stick in farewell. I asked him what he had done to his leg and he stopped and looked down at it and then looked up at me again in incredulity.

'Would you believe it,' he said. 'I must have run hundreds of miles over the past year, and then I sprain my ankle getting out of a taxi.'

The conference was being held in a suburb by the sea, whose dockyards were so extensive that the bright-blue water remained hidden behind mile after mile of warehouses and silos and giant stacks of shipping containers. Enormous cranes loaded or unloaded the colourful rectangles one by one from the deserted decks of vast tankers that waited amid the concrete expanses of the dockside.

The hotel was a grey block surrounded by other, taller blocks of apartments, all of whose windows remained covered day and night by metal shutters. Directly in front of the hotel was a car park. Several flagpoles stood erect in a line in the tarmac and their wires made a singing sound in the wind like that of a ship's rigging. On the right-hand side a bank of dry grass rose up to meet a wall with some overgrown trees – cedars and eucalyptus – behind it. They formed a neglected avenue along what appeared to be an old driveway made of dusty white earth that curved around to meet a pair of rusty gates ornately fashioned out of iron, and then continued beyond them, disappearing into the trees around the hillside where a wedge of glittering sea could just be seen below. The gates were locked and the earth around them was so undisturbed it suggested they had not been opened in a long time.

The conference was held at this hotel year after year, one of the delegates told me, despite the fact that it was ugly and also inconvenient, being a long way from the centre and with little in the way of transport links. He supposed the organisers had a deal with the manager. At mealtimes all the delegates had to be loaded into a bus and driven for twenty minutes through the featureless, broken-down suburbs to a restaurant, where he supposed they had another deal. The restaurant, he added, was actually very good, since eating in this country was a national sport, but the problem was that the deal – whatever it was – involved a set menu, so you were surrounded by people feasting on a whole variety of delicacies while being given no choice in what to eat yourself. More than once he had seen the organisers proudly lead a group of delegates outside – where chefs were cooking fresh fish and great skewers of squid and prawns on enormous braziers – in order to take photographs of the scene, before being returned inside to face the same meagre panoply of soup and cold cuts they'd been offered the day before. The hotel itself provided only tea and coffee, but somewhere hidden in that concrete shoe-box or its environs, he said, was a pastry chef of rare talent, and he urged me to try one of the small tarts that were usually circulated with the hot drinks in the breaks between sessions. These tarts were a common element of the national fare, he said, and could be bought in mass-produced form from supermarkets, but not since childhood had he tasted an example to match those on offer here. He had almost forgotten, so ubiquitous were the copies, that the original had ever existed, and it almost gave him pain to re-enter the colour and texture and savour of that lost authen-ticity, which was not, he felt almost certain, the work of a professional team but of someone working, as it were, alone. He had never, however, in his years of coming here, glimpsed that person, nor even made an effort to enquire about him or her; he merely knew, when he bit into one of the fresh, delicious tarts, that they were unmistakably the work of the same indi-vidual. There had been an English delegate here once who had claimed to have had the same epiphany with a national sweet – it was called, he believed, the Eccles cake – and this man's remarks had caused him to wonder whether something of the lost mother wasn't being sought in that case, because for himself it was merely a question of art. The original recipe for the tart, it was said, had been devised by nuns who used such quantities of egg whites to starch their habits that they had to think of something to do with all the yolks. A convent would not be one's first port of call in search of the maternal, that much was true; and he had even wondered whether this tart of the nuns, to which the citizens of their nation – especially the men – were virtually addicted, symbolised something about the country's attitude to women. When he thought of those habits, so stiff and white and pure, it occurred to him that they were the vestments of sexlessness and of a life without men. The sweet little tart, by which the man's hungry mouth was fobbed off and occupied, was perhaps nothing less than these women's divested femininity, separated and handed over, as it were, on a plate; a method of keeping the world at bay as well as a sign, he liked to think, of the happiness of that state, for he didn't believe that anything created in suffering and self-abnegation could taste quite so delicious.

The hotel had a long central corridor on each floor with a row of rooms to either side. The floors were all identical, with brown carpets and beige walls and rooms standing in a row along the corridors in exactly the same sequence. There were two big stainless steel lifts that rose and fell slowly, the doors continuously opening and closing in the reception lobby, where people sat on plain red sofas apparently mes-

126

merised by the endlessly repeating spectacle of one set of doors closing on a human group while the other set of doors released a new group. Sometimes, in the corridors on the upper floors, the doors to the rooms stood open while they were being cleaned and it could be seen that they were all the same, with the same brown carpet and shiny laminated-wood furniture and the same view of the surrounding apartment blocks with their shuttered windows. Yet on those occasions when a guest was to be seen letting themselves into their room with the hotel's plastic key card, something in their demeanour suggested they unconsciously believed their own room to be recognisable and distinct. The cleaners wore white aprons and worked all hours of the day, moving steadily along the corridors and up and down the floors and back again. They had big plastic-wrapped bundles of starched white bed linen that they left piled outside in the corridors while they worked inside the rooms, so that the corridor sometimes looked like a deserted landscape where snow has just fallen.

Downstairs in the reception area there was a large television screen surrounded by sofas where groups of men often sat or stood to watch a few minutes of football or Formula One racing. When the news came on the men usually wandered away, so that the news-reader would be left earnestly addressing an empty space. Directly on the other side of the big plate-glass windows was the smoking area, where more groups of men and the occasional woman stood, mirroring the group around the television inside. These two spaces were also where the delegates tended to gather before an event or to take the bus to the restaurant, and on those occasions the presence of the large panes of glass between one group of delegates and another – each able to see but not hear the other – seemed to signify something about the artificiality of our situation. A little further along there was a bench which faced away from the hotel, looking out over the parked cars, and which seemed to have been elected as a place for solitude, despite the fact that it stood just on the other side of the windows and could be clearly seen from inside. The people on the sofas were no more than a foot or two away from the person on the bench, the back of whose head they could see in great detail. Nevertheless, when someone sat on that bench it was understood they wished to be alone or to be approached singly and with caution, whereupon a much quieter and lengthier conversation than those in which the group was generally engaged could ensue. It was here also that people often made telephone calls, speaking in other languages than the English that was generally the currency of conversation.

The organisers of the conference wore T-shirts printed

with the conference logo and were mostly very young. They gave an appearance of constant watchfulness and anxiety, since it was their responsibility to make sure that everyone attended their events or caught the bus, and were often to be seen locked in sombre consultation, their eyes glancing frequently around the hotel lobby as they talked. If a delegate was absent there were frantic searches and lengthy narratives concerning when he or she had last been seen. Often one of the organisers would go up in the lift to search upstairs, whereupon the doors of the other lift would not infrequently open to reveal the missing delegate. One of the other writers present, a Welsh novelist, was the cause of constant anxiety for his habit of setting off on foot into the undistinguished labyrinth of the surrounding suburbs and returning with stories of churches or other distant landmarks he had visited. He wore walking boots and always carried a small knapsack, as though to remind the organisers of the tenuousness of their hold on him, and indeed he had several times failed to present himself at mealtimes for the bus, only to appear at the restaurant slightly flushed and breathless but nonetheless punctual, having walked there from somewhere else. This same man went to great lengths to befriend other participants – organisers and delegates alike – writing down the particulars of things they said or places they talked about in a small creased leather notebook and frequently returning to them to check that he'd noted the name of a town or book or restaurant correctly. He told me that he always made such notes on his travels, typing them up and filing them according to name and date when he got home, so that he only had to open the file on, say, his visit to the Frankfurt book fair three years earlier for every one of its details to be available to him. He had got into this habit, which more or less dispensed with the necessity for remembering anything, not because he tended to be forgetful but because his capacity for holding on to information, however useless or trivial, would otherwise have kept him in a state of constant distraction. It was apparent that his conversational tactic of asking people questions – which he appeared to adopt, though he didn't say so, out of shyness – made him the recipient of an unusual amount of such information, and yet when asked a question about himself he would become evasive and vague and unwilling to go into more than the sketchiest detail about his circumstances. He had, he said, attended every single event at the conference, even those conducted in languages he didn't understand: he felt the organisers would have been disappointed in him otherwise.

I noticed that while the Welsh novelist talked lengthily to everyone with a minor or tangential connection to himself – including the driver of the bus and the hotel staff – he tended to avoid those he might have considered his equals, well-known writers from his own and other countries. There were several of these in attendance, some of whom I had met before, including one who approached me on the second day and reminded me that we had once participated in an all-female panel discussion together in Amsterdam, in which the panellists – distinguished female thinkers and intellectuals – had been asked to talk about their dreams. I remembered her on that occasion as timid and strained-looking with a somewhat indignant air, but standing in the hotel lobby she emanated poise and vigour, as though in the years since we'd last met she'd been acquiring energy rather than expending it, and she reminded me of her name – which was Sophia – with the pragmatic directness of someone who accepts rather than fears the likelihood of such things being forgotten. I can't imagine, she said now with a gracious smile, a panel of male intellectuals being asked to discuss their dreams, and I suppose the moderator was hoping to elicit our so-called honesty; as though, she said, a woman's relationship to truth were at best unconscious, when in fact it might sim- ply be the case that female truth – if such a thing can even be said to exist – is so interior and involuted that a common version of it can never be agreed on. It's

131

a saddening thought, she said, that when a group of women get together, far from advancing the cause of femininity, they end up pathologising it.

Since our evening in Amsterdam she had published several novels, she told me, as well as a book about the Western literary canon, from which she had argued numerous men should be removed and numerous women added. That book had been well received elsewhere, she said, but here in her native country it had virtually been ignored. She was attending this conference not on account of her credentials as a feminist writer but for her work as a translator, by which she had enabled several of this country's writers – nearly all of them men – to become more internationally recognised than she was herself. Or maybe, she said, with a high bell-like laugh, I'm only here because this is my hometown. They have to fly everyone else in from all over the place, she said, but it's cheap to invite me because I only have to walk up the road.

I wondered whether the fact that she was at home was the explanation for her altered appearance, as though she shone more brightly in her natural setting. She wore a tight, low-cut dress in a vivid turquoise colour, with a broad belt cinched to emphasise the slenderness of her waist, and a matching pair of high-heeled boots. She was very small and slight, with sallow skin and thin, soft, light-brown hair and a large expressive mouth, and she held her head up very high, like a child standing on tiptoe and straining to see over the adults. Around her throat and wrist she wore several pieces of jewellery and her face was carefully made up, especially around the eyes, which she had outlined dramatically so that they appeared continually startled, as though they were observing things whose intensity and extremity only she could see. After a while I could recognise behind this disguise the timid woman I remembered, and I understood her outfit to be something designed to prevent her from being forgotten or ignored, yet it also had the effect of making her femininity seem a kind of question other people were required to answer or a problem they were expected to solve.

This was not, she said, gesturing through the plate-glass doors, in all honesty the most exciting place to live, but after her divorce she had recognised that it would be better for her and her son to be near her parents, and so they had left the capital, though she hoped to return there one day, she said, once the dust had settled.

'My mother is very kind to us,' she said, 'despite the fact that I am the first member of my family to get divorced and that this is a stigma on her, which she can't quite bring herself to let me forget. She looks at my son when she knows I am watching her and she puts her hand over her mouth as if some priceless object had just fallen to the floor and smashed to pieces in front of her eyes. She treats him like he has a terrible illness,' she said, 'and perhaps he has, but if so it's up to him to survive it, even if other people are sympathetic to him.'

The child had in fact recently broken his leg playing football, she went on, and the injury had mysteriously developed into a viral infection whose cause or cure the doctors couldn't seem to find. He was in hospital for a month and bedridden for two months after that, and this experience had brought about a profound change in his character, she said, because he had always been very physically active and obsessed with sport, from whose rules and rewards he had seemed to take his ethos for living. As the witness of his parents' divorce, for instance, he was forever trying to figure out which side he should be on, and who had won and who lost in each of the many battles being played out before his eyes. It was natural, obviously, for him to side with his father, with whose male values he identified and with whom moreover he did many of the activities he enjoyed; and his father had shown little restraint in exploiting that loyalty at every opportunity, inculcating in him as he did so the beginnings of a much greater tribal identity by which, she could see, the child's entire life and character would be shaped. That tribe was one to which nearly all the men in this country belonged, and it defined itself through a fear of women combined with an utter dependence on them; and so despite her best efforts it was only a matter of time, she realised, before her son's questions about right and wrong found their answer in the low-level bigotry with which he was surrounded and to which everything was encouraging him to submit. Nevertheless, whenever he complained that his father had said one thing and she another, she refused to offer an opinion on which of them was right, as he was imploring her to. Make up your own mind, she would say; use your brain. He would often become upset by her response, and this was the proof that her ex-husband was giving him the most partisan accounts of their situation, because the child simply couldn't cope when there was no side for him to be on; in other words, when there was no point of view. Yet the effort of using his brain was far less appealing than the easy prospect of believing his father's stories; that is, until he was physically immobilised for a three-month period.

In bed he had entered what at first seemed to be depression, becoming silent and listless and struggling to show an interest in anything, and this was followed by a period of anger and frustration which, though different, was just as bad. Incapacitated as he was, and removed from the field of action, the facts of his life became much clearer to him. One of those facts was that his father rarely called or came to see him; another was that his mother was never far from his bedside. One morning, she said, I came into his room with some breakfast for him on a tray. I had been up working since six o'clock because I had a piece to deliver later that day, and I hadn't yet showered or brushed my hair. I was wearing my glasses and my oldest clothes and I didn't have any make-up on, and he looked up at me from the bed and he said to me, Mama, you look so ugly. And I said yes, this is what I look like sometimes. At other times I wear make-up and nice clothes and I look pretty, but this is also what I am like. I don't always please you, I said, but I am just as real this way as the other way.

She paused and turned her eyes through the windows towards the car park, where the other delegates could be seen gathering for the bus. The wind blew their hair sideways and flattened their clothes against their bodies.

When he got out of bed, she continued presently, he was a quieter and more thoughtful person, and he even accepted the news that he would not be able to play any sport for at least another year with good grace. In a way I am grateful, she said, for his illness, even though at the time it felt like the last straw and as if there was no end to my bad luck. It seemed so unfair, she said, that while his father was driving around in his sports-car and visiting his girlfriend at her villa on the coast, I was stuck in a tiny flat in my hometown with a sick child and my mother calling five times a day to tell me it was all my fault for being too outspoken and continuing to work after I got married. In this country, she said, the only power women recognise is the power of the slave, and the only justice they understand is the slave's fatalistic justice. At least she loves my son, she said, although I've noticed that the people who love children the most often respect them the least.

A tall, bulky, sombre-looking man had entered the lobby and was standing not far from us looking absorbedly at his phone. With his thick black curly hair and black beard and large pouchy immobile face, he looked like one of the giant, pitted statues of Roman antiquity. When she noticed him Sophia's face lit up and she darted forward to touch his arm, whereupon he looked slowly up from the screen with a marked unwillingness, while his large, faintly sorrowful eyes registered the nature of the interruption. Sophia spoke to him trillingly and rapidly in her native language and he replied slowly and sonorously, standing quite still while she became very animated, her posture constantly changing and her hands gesturing and fluttering while she talked. He was much taller than her and held his head very erect so that when he looked down at her his eyes appeared to be half-closed, which gave the impression that he was either bored or mesmerised by their conversation. After a while she turned to me, and laying her hand once more on his arm, introduced the man as Luís. He is our most important novelist at this moment, she added, while his head lifted even further and his eyes threatened to close entirely. This year he has won all five of our major literary prizes for his latest book. It has been a sensation, she said, because the subjects Luís writes about are subjects our other male writers would not deign to touch.

I was surprised to hear this assessment of Luís, after Sophia's earlier remarks about male writers and their tendency to eclipse her, and I asked what subjects those were.

Domesticity, Sophia said very earnestly, and the ordinary life of the suburbs, the ordinary men and women and children who live there. These were things, she reiterated, that most writers would consider to be beneath them, pursuing instead the fantastical or the noteworthy, gathering around themes of public importance in the hope, she didn't doubt, of increasing their own importance by doing so. Yet Luís had trounced them all with his simplicity, his honesty, his reverence for reality.

I write about what I know, Luís said, shrugging and looking over our heads at something in the distance.

He is being modest, Sophia said with her bell-like laugh, because he worries he would betray the world he writes about by becoming arrogant. Yet in fact he has given it a new dignity, one that is unique in our culture, where the divisions between rich and poor, between young and old, and most of all between men and women have seemed insurmountable. We live with an almost superstitious belief in our own differences, she said, and Luís has shown that those differences are not the result of some divine mystery but are merely the consequence of our lack of empathy, which if we had it would enable us to see that in fact we are all the same. It is for his empathy, she said, that Luís has received such acclaim, and so I believe he should congratulate himself, rather than feeling ashamed for being praised.

Luís looked most unhappy while all this was being said, and his response was a profound silence that lasted until the organisers called us to the bus that had drawn up outside. We drove along wide, empty roads whose pale concrete surfaces were fissured and cracked and thronged with weeds, circumnavigating the strange, unpeopled landscape of the vast dock, whose block-like impenetrable shapes extended as far as the eye could see, and then re-entering the shabby, discursive network of suburban streets on the other side. The day was grey and windy beneath a low sky, so that where the human dimension appeared it looked fretted and oppressed: the awnings of restaurants and shops were flapping, litter was bowling along the pavements, the breeze was tugging hanks of smoke from outdoor braziers into the air, scattered groups of pedestrians were clutching their bags and coats and pressing forward with bowed heads. When we arrived at the street where the restaurant was, it was blocked: the road had been entirely dug up since the day before, and was now a trench marked off by incident tape that snapped and fluttered in the wind. The bus manoeuvred its way into a side street and then made a lengthy series of slow turns, while its occupants discussed this new development, eventually dismissing it with head-shaking and resigned shrugs. Finally the bus found a place some distance from the restaurant to let us off, and people began to walk alone or in groups back to where we had been. We passed through a concrete lot surrounded by decrepit graffitied buildings, where laurel trees were putting out their red spiky flowers. A strange music came in eddies on the wind from somewhere nearby: it was the sound of someone playing a pipe or flute, and presently a boy could be seen standing half-concealed in the shrubbery in the ruins of a graffitied wall, the instrument lifted to his lips.

It was typical, the man beside me said as we clambered over the makeshift walkway that had been put up over the former street, that these roadworks should have appeared without warning and apparently by magic, when the organisers could have chosen one of any number of restaurants in the area for us to visit three times each day, and one should be slow, he said, to attribute this inconvenience to a lack of information, because it was quite possible the organisers knew about it all along but were unwilling to change their arrangements. It would be easy to believe, he said, that the people of this country were beset by feelings of powerlessness, but it could just as well be called stubbornness, because they refused to change even when change was a possibility. He himself worked for their most important national newspaper and had had frequent opportunities to see this phenomenon at first hand: one day he would be sent to cover a major political crisis or human disaster and the next to report on the supposed appearance of the Virgin Mary on a rock somewhere in the countryside, and would be expected to treat these two events with equal seriousness. Just as there might be an explanation for the appearance of the roadworks, he said, so there ought to be for the lady in blue: you can't have one without the other, he said, and so people accept the mystery of the roadworks as a way of avoiding asking themselves the bigger questions.

We had entered the restaurant by now and had sat down at the long table reserved for the delegates that stretched all along one side of the room. The other side was always crowded, and the noise and laughter that emanated from there contrasted with the awkward-ness of the long table and the fixity of its set places, to which the delegates were increasingly reluctant to consign themselves, knowing their fate would thus be settled for the duration of the meal, and against which they had started to make pacts before crossing the threshold as to who would sit where. Only a few feet away on the other side of the room people were gath-ered in noisy, ebullient groups, embroiled in meals that appeared to have no beginning and no end and to which the waiters, threading through the crowds with dishes borne on silver trays above their heads, kept adding more and more developments.

The man beside me unfurled his thick white nap-kin with a flourish and tucked it into the collar of his shirt. He was somewhere in his sixties, with a bald nut-brown head and an expression of cynical humour in his small round eyes. He had read my book, he said, and would be interviewing me for his news-paper, but in considering what to say to me a novel idea had occurred to him, which was to treat me as one of my own characters, with himself granted the power of narrator. This was not the kind of approach he generally adopted in literary interviews, of which he had done a perhaps excessive number, considering all the other matters he was expected to cover for the paper: tomorrow, for instance, he had to attend the cup final, an irksome assignment since he found the crowds and their mad excitement over something that after all happened without fail every year particularly tiresome, and as he had said he had often found himself writing about religious miracles one day and state corruption the next. Interviews with literary authors he usually enjoyed, but all the same he saw it as his task to bring himself to their world, researching their lives and reading their previous work and generally boning up on the issues they concerned themselves with. But this time, perhaps because he had been so busy and because there were so many authors at the conference requiring his attention, he had approached my book without much in the way of context. In fact he had only finished it late last night, returning to his room after dinner, and it was as he was going to sleep that the idea of acting as its author had come to him. It interested him that he had been led to believe he could assume that power: usually novels had the opposite effect on him, in that he couldn't ever imagine writing as the author had written, or indeed, in some cases, wanting to; even thinking about it exhausted him, and he sometimes found himself wishing these prodigies had a little less energy, because every time they wrote something new they also created his obligation to respond to it. The tremendous effort to conjure something out of nothing, to create this great structure of language where before there had been only blankness, was something of which he personally felt himself incapable: it usually rendered him, in fact, quite passive and left him feeling relieved to return to the trivial details of his own life. He had noticed, for instance, that my characters were often provoked into feats of self-revelation by means of a simple question, and that had obviously led him to consider his own occupation, of which the asking of questions was a central feature. Yet his questions rarely elicited such mellifluous replies: in fact, he usually found himself praying that his interviewee would say something interesting, because otherwise it would be left to him to make a newsworthy piece out of it. Going to sleep, as he had said, he had suddenly felt inexplicably empowered in that regard, as though he had realised a far simpler question than those he usually asked – and perhaps, indeed, only one – would unlock the whole mystery for him. The question he liked the most – and this was the one he intended to ask me, in his new role as narrator – concerned what I had noticed on my way here, and if his – or rather my – theory was correct, by asking me that question, the question of what I had noticed on my way here, he would enable me to write the whole interview for him, so to speak.

Two men had sat down opposite us at the table, and one of them now interrupted to ask whether he had heard correctly that my neighbour was going to cover the cup final tomorrow; and if so, what his opinions were on the likely outcome. My neighbour slowly and painstakingly readjusted the napkin in the collar of his shirt, and with an expression of sombre patience began to give a long and apparently regretful reply, whose import seemed to be that it would not be the outcome they wished for. A heated discussion ensued, during which Sophia entered the restaurant and, seeing an empty place beside mine, came and sat down in it. In that same moment Luís – who had followed her in – could be seen striding towards the other end of the table and then bypassing it entirely, taking a seat alone at a small table in the very furthest corner of the restaurant. Sophia gave a little gasp of frustration and, standing up again, said that she was just going to find out why Luís was insisting on sitting alone. She returned a few minutes later and regretfully picked up her bag, saying that since he wouldn't move she would have to go and keep him company, as she felt it was wrong to let him go off like that. My neighbour broke off from his conversation to tell her that this was a ridiculous proposition: what are you doing, he said, adjusting again the white napkin in the collar of his shirt and looking at her with his small, round, inquisitive eyes, pursuing him around the restaurant? If Luís wanted to be alone, he should be left that way; otherwise he should come and join the rest of us. Sophia considered this with a delicately knitted brow and then trod lightly off in her high-heeled boots, this time returning after some minutes with a truculent-looking Luís in tow.

'We won't allow this depressive behaviour,' she said to him with her trilling laugh. 'We're going to keep you in the land of the living.'

Luís sat down with an expression of undisguised irritation on his face and promptly joined the other men in discussing football, whereupon Sophia turned to me and meekly said into my ear that while she realised Luís could give the impression of being arrogant, in fact his success was painful for him and caused him to suffer from intense guilt, as well as from feelings of overexposure.

'Unusually for a man of this nation,' she said, 'and perhaps for any man, he has been honest about his own life. He has written about his family and his parents and his childhood home in a way that makes them completely recognisable, and because this is a small country he worries he has used them or compromised them, though of course for readers in other parts of the world it is just the honesty itself that comes through. Though of course if he were a woman,' she said, leaning more confidentially towards my ear, 'he would be scorned for his honesty, or at the very least no one would care.'

She sat back so that the waiters could put the dishes on the table. They contained a brown, strong-smelling puree, and Sophia wrinkled her nose and said that this dish had a name that could more or less be translated as 'the parts no one would eat otherwise'. She took a tiny spoonful and dabbed it on the edge of her plate. The Welsh novelist had by now appeared, his hair stiffened by the wind and his shirt unbuttoned to show his flushed neck. After some hesitation he sat down in the only remaining seat, beside Sophia, smiling warily to show his narrow yellow teeth. When he asked her what was in the dishes, she did not repeat her translation but merely smiled graciously and said that it was a local delicacy made of ground meat. He reached forward and piled some on to his plate, as well as several pieces of bread. We would have to excuse him, he said: he was extremely hungry, having attempted to walk out along the coast and instead become increasingly entangled in a series of industrial complexes and housing developments and shopping precincts, all of which appeared to be in a state of semi-ruin and were more or less deserted, yet to which all roads unerringly led, so that finally he was forced to clamber over walls and verges in the attempt to get to the water, finding himself at last in a cordoned-off concrete expanse surrounded by barbed wire and what looked like numerous watchtowers, being held at gunpoint by three men in uniform. He had wandered, apparently, into a military zone, and it took all his scant linguistic resources to explain to these men that he was not a terrorist but a writer attending the literary conference, of which – perhaps surprisingly – they had heard. They turned out to be quite genial, and offered him coffee and tarts before sending him on his way, which he regretted not having accepted once he'd realised how far he was from the restaurant. He'd had to run most of the way back, he said, which in his walking boots was no easy feat.

Luís's attention had been caught by this narrative and he launched into an account of the country's socio-economic decline, which had been precipitated, he said, by the financial crisis nearly a decade earlier whose reverberations, in places like this one, were still being felt. The Welsh novelist used this diversion as the opportunity to eat, nodding his head frequently while he despatched his first course and then, satisfied, sitting back in his chair. His own region of Wales, he said when Luís had finished speaking, was similarly on a more or less unrelievedly downward trajectory, though it had barely completed its evolution into the modern era in the first place. There were still families, he said, where only a generation earlier the elders had spoken no English, and in his conversations with local people he heard of a world in which humans had once lived deeply and richly in their own habitat, on familiar terms not just with one another but also with animals, birds, mountains and trees, as well as with traditions of song and storytelling and worship, and of emotional histories too, of deep grudges and unbreachable rifts, of clans that married and intermarried, dwelling on the land in a reality all their own. Not forty years ago, he said, whole communities would climb the mountain together on Sundays, old ladies and babes in arms, strapping farmers and village girls and chattering gangs of children, along with their dogs and ponies and baskets of food, of ham sandwiches and great thermoses of tea, and the men would sing as they climbed the hill. The novel he was currently writing was an attempt to revive that vanished world, and he had done considerable research into its manners and mores, as well as its agricultural practices, its culinary and domestic traditions, its patterns of churchgoing and socialising, its folklore, its vernacular poetry and song. He had interviewed countless people, most of them – for obvious reasons –

elderly, and had built up a quite extraordinary picture in terms of his preparatory notes, yet what was surprising was how often these people claimed to be relieved not to live in that way any longer, even as they expressed their nostalgia for it. Sometimes he almost thought he felt the loss of the old world more keenly than they did themselves, because he actually didn't see how they could bear the drabness of their old people's homes with their gutless conveniences of television and central heating, when what they remembered was so beautiful. Nothing remained, one old lady had said to him, of the world she knew: not one blade of grass was the same. He had asked her to explain what she meant, because surely grass was at least still grass, but she had merely repeated that over the course of her lifetime every single thing had changed and become unrecognisable to her. This lady had died peacefully not long after his conversation with her, and he felt lucky, he said, to have had the chance to speak to her and record her memories, which otherwise would have died with her. Yet even as he reconstructed those memories, so painstakingly that they shone like new in the pages of his novel, the meaning of her remarks about change continued to elude him. He could not, in the end, accept that the very essence of things had been lost, and at times he had almost become angry with her while writing, as though it was she herself who had stolen that essence and taken it away with her for good. Where he lived, for instance – in a farmhouse in the Snowdonia national park – the landscape was more or less unaltered and the local community were very active in combatting the small changes – excessive road signage, new car parks – that by increments would damage its character and beauty, as well as in reviving some of the old cottage industries and traditions of land management. When he walked out into those hills, their reality, he believed, was just as it had always been, though of course, he added, glancing warily around at the others, he realised he was fortunate to live somewhere of which that could be said.

Luís had been listening with an impassive expression on his great moody face, his fingers occupied with tearing small sections from a piece of bread and rolling them into hard little balls which he then dropped on the table around his plate.

'My mother once told me,' he said, 'that at harvest time when she was a child the village held a day of festival, and the farmers would always leave one last field to mow on that day. Everyone would stand to watch the men mowing with their scythes, because this was a tradition, and it was also a tradition that they left a circular patch in the middle of the field unmown, working in from the edges of the field rather than up and down in straight lines as they usually did. All of the frightened wildlife that normally had the opportunity to run away was therefore trapped in this circle,' he said, 'which got smaller and smaller as the men mowed around it, so that in the end there were a great number of creatures cowering there. The village children had already been armed with shovels and picks and even knives from the kitchen, and at a certain moment they were permitted to come forward and descend on the unmown circle in a cheering mob to kill the animals, which they did with great pleasure and gusto, spattering themselves and each other with blood. My mother cannot think about these episodes,' he said, 'without becoming upset, even though at the time she participated in them quite happily, and indeed many of our relations now deny that such barbaric practices ever occurred. But my mother says that they did, and she continues to suffer on account of them, because unlike the others she has remained honest, and she refuses to remember the past without also remembering its cruelty. I sometimes wonder,' he said, 'whether she believes she sealed her own fate with that unthinking conduct, because life has treated her cruelly in return, yet it is only her sensitivity that creates that impression and her relatives, as I have said, don't see things that way at all. When I started to write,' he said, 'it was because I felt the pressure of her sensitivity, as though it was an affliction or unfinished task I had to take from her, or something she had bequeathed to me that I had to fulfil. Yet in my own life I have been as doomed to repetition as anyone else, even when I didn't know what it was I was repeating.'

'But that is completely untrue,' Sophia exclaimed. 'Your life has been completely transformed by your talents and what you have made of them – you can go anywhere and meet anyone, your praises are sung all over the world, you have your nice apartment in the city, you even have a wife,' she said with a pleasant smile, 'that you don't have to live with and who is devoted to bringing up your child. If you were a woman you would certainly find your mother's life hanging over your head like a sword and you would be asking yourself what progress you had made, other than to double for yourself the work she had been expected to do and receive three times the blame for it.'

The waiters had by now removed the dishes of puree and were bringing the next course, a small moulded shape which Sophia portentously described as being made of fish, and of which she again took only the tiniest amount. When the dish was passed to Luís he waved it away and sat hunched and unoccupied in his chair, staring at the wall above our heads, where various nautical items – fishing nets, giant brass hooks, the wooden steering wheel of a boat – had been hung

153

as decorations. It was interesting, Sophia said now to the Welsh novelist, that he had repeated those words of the old lady, because she had recently heard almost exactly the same words herself, although in a very different context. Her son had not long ago gone to stay for a few days with his father, and had come upon a cache of photograph albums he had never seen before. Her ex-husband had taken all the photograph albums when they separated, she explained, perhaps because he believed he owned their history or perhaps because there was something in those albums he feared would contradict his version of what happened, because otherwise, she said, why would he hide them away?

'Whatever the reason,' she said, 'he left me with not one single photograph of our life together, and so when my son found the albums in a cupboard he was in a way seeing that life for the first time, since much of it he was too young to remember. When he came home after the visit,' she said, 'I could see straight away that something had happened, and he was very quiet for several hours. He kept looking at me when he thought I wouldn't notice, and in the end I said to him, have I got something on my face? Is that why you keep looking at me in that strange way? So then he told me about finding the albums, which he spent the whole morning going through, because his father had gone out to play tennis with some friends and had left him alone. You are in the pictures, Mama, he said to me, except it isn't actually you. I mean, he said, I know the person in the pictures was you, but I couldn't recognise you. I told him I hadn't seen those photographs for years,' Sophia said, 'but that I must have aged more than I thought I had. No, he said to me, it isn't that you look older. It's that everything about you has changed. Nothing is the same as in the photographs, he said, not your hair or your clothes or your expression, not even your eyes.'

While she spoke her eyes grew larger and more brilliant and it seemed possible they were filling with tears, yet she continued to smile in a way that made it clear she was practised in keeping her composure. The Welsh novelist looked at her with polite concern, an expression of faint alarm on his face.

'Poor kid,' Luís said gloomily. 'Why does this bastard arrange a tennis match in the first place?'

'Because that way,' Sophia said, smiling more graciously than ever, 'he knows he deprives me of my freedom and peace of mind even when I have some time to myself. If he took care of our son during their weekends together,' she said, 'he would in a sense be giving something to me, and he has devoted his life to making sure that is something he will never do, even through the medium of our child. I have no doubt,' she said, 'that if our son was wholly in his care he would do a first-rate job of bringing him up, making sure he beat all the other boys at sport and won at every competition and punished his mother regularly with his lack of concern for her. In court,' she said, 'he fought me for custody, and I know that many of my friends were shocked that I opposed it, because they thought that as a feminist I ought to promote equality for both sides, and also because there is the belief that a son needs his father in some special way, to learn how to be a man. But I don't want my son to learn to be a man,' she said. 'I want him to become one through experience. I want him to find out how to act, how to treat a woman, how to think for himself. I don't want him learning to drop his underwear on the floor,' she said, 'or using his male nature as an excuse.'

The Welsh novelist raised a finger hesitantly and said that he hated to disagree, but that he felt it was important to point out that not all men would behave as her ex-husband had done, and that male values were not merely the product of enshrined selfishness but could include such things as honour, duty and chivalry. He himself had two sons, as well as a daughter, and he liked to think they were well-balanced individuals. He couldn't deny, he said, that there were differences between the girl and the boys, and that likewise to deny the differences between men and women was perhaps to obviate the best qualities of both. He recognised he was very lucky in that he and his wife had a good marriage, and he found that their differences were generally complementary, rather than the source of conflict.

'Is your wife also a writer?' Luís said, toying indifferently with his napkin.

His wife was a full-time mother, the Welsh novelist said, and both of them were satisfied with that arrangement, since his literary revenue very fortunately meant that she didn't have to earn money and could instead help him find the time he needed to work. In fact, he said, she did do a bit of writing in her spare time and had recently written a book for children that had been quite a surprise hit. When their children were smaller she used to tell them stories involving a Welsh pony called Gwendolyn, and in the end there were so many of these stories, all following one from the other so as to keep the children's attention night after night, that the book, she had said, literally wrote itself. Obviously he himself was too subjective to be able to offer an opinion on the adventures of Gwendolyn, but he had shown it to his agent, who had luckily been able to find his wife a pretty impressive three-book deal.

'My ex-wife and I used to tell my son stories,' Luís said gloomily, 'and of course we read to him in bed every night, but it hasn't made the slightest difference. He doesn't pick up a book from one day to the next. Sometimes he has to read something for school and it is as if he is being tortured, yet when I was his age I read everything I could get my hands on, including the instructions for the washing machine and my mother's gossip magazines, because there were no books in the house. But my son is repelled, to the extent that he is always losing the book he's meant to be reading. I'll find it lying outside in the rain, or forgotten in the pocket of his coat or beside the bath, and each time I'll retrieve it and clean it up and replace it where he can find it, because I see in the rejection of these books a rejection of myself and of my authority as a father. My son loves me,' he said, 'and he doesn't consciously blame me for the things that have happened to him, but I suspect he feels that if he gave his attention to a book and lost himself in it, he might never be found again, and the world he is trying to hold on to might spin out of his control. My ex-wife and I treat him with the utmost kindness,' he said, 'and we have done everything in our power to get along with one another since our separation and to reassure him that he was not the cause of it, but his response has been to show absolutely no curiosity about life and to anchor himself by means of his own reliable comforts and pleasures. He sits in his room day after day, motivated to do nothing but watch television and eat pastries and other sweets, and it is impossible not to feel,' he said, 'that we have broken him, not out of malice but out of our own carelessness and selfishness.'

Sophia, who had been becoming increasingly agitated while Luís spoke, now interrupted him.

'But you aren't helping him,' she said, 'by treating him as a fragile thing and shielding him and covering up your conflict, when the consequences of that conflict are right in front of him every day. I couldn't protect my son,' she said, 'and so instead he has had to make up his own mind and to realise that his destiny is in his own hands. When he doesn't want to read a book I say to him, fine, if your choice is to work in the gas station out on the highway when you grow up, then don't read it. Children have to survive hardship,' she said, while Luís sombrely shook his head, 'and you have to let them, because otherwise they will never be strong.'

By now the waiters had brought the final course, an oily fish stew of which no one except the Welsh novelist had eaten very much. Luís looked with a harrowed expression at Sophia, and sadly pushed his plate away from him as if it were the offer of her optimism and determination.

'They are wounded,' he said slowly. 'Wounded, and I don't know why this particular wound has been so deadly in the case of my son, but since I gave him the wound it is my job to tend him. All I know,' he said, 'is that I'm not telling the story any more, either to him or to myself.'

There was a silence while the waiters cleared the dishes, and even the men opposite, who had sustained a conversation about the leadership qualities of José Mourinho for all this time, stopped talking and gazed ahead of them with blank, satiated expressions.

'I have known many men,' Sophia said, resting her slender arms on the table, whose white cloth was littered with crumpled napkins and wine stains and half-eaten pieces of bread, 'from many different parts of the world, and the men of this nation,' she said, blinking her painted eyes and smiling, 'are the sweetest but also the most childlike. Behind every man is his mother,' she said, 'who made so much fuss of him he will never recover from it, and will never understand why the rest of the world doesn't make the same fuss of him, particularly the woman who has replaced his mother and who he can neither trust nor forgive for replacing her. These men like nothing better than to have a child,' she said, 'because then the whole cycle is repeated and they feel comfortable. Men from other places are different,' she said, 'but in the end neither better nor worse: they are better lovers but less courteous, or they are more confident but less considerate. The English man,' she said, looking at me, 'is in my experience the worst, because he is neither a skilled lover nor a sweet child, and because his idea of a woman is something made of plastic not flesh. The English man is sent away from his mother, and so he wants to marry his mother and perhaps even to be his mother, and while he is usually polite and reasonable to women, as a stranger would be, he doesn't understand what they are.

'After my son found the photographs in his father's house,' she went on, 'and made the observation that I was not the same person I had been, not even in the molecules of my skin, I became for a while very confused and depressed. It suddenly felt as if all my efforts since the divorce to keep things the same, to keep my own life recognisable to me and to my son, were in fact false, because underneath the surface not one thing remained as it was. Yet his words also made me feel that for the first time someone had understood what had happened, because while I had always told the story to myself and others as a story of war, in fact it was simply a story of change. And it was this change that had been left unexamined and unremarked on, until my son saw it in the photographs and noticed it. While he was away for those few days visiting his father,' she said, 'I had arranged to spend time with a man and had invited him for the weekend to our apartment. I have had to be careful about allowing my son to see me with other men, for the reason that he might innocently mention something to his father, who would undoubtedly respond with the most vitriolic aggression. This necessity for caution and secrecy,' she said, 'has also made these interludes of passion more exciting: they are a kind of reward I offer myself, and I often spend time thinking about them and planning them, even sometimes when I am with my son and for whatever reason am feeling bored. But on this occasion,' she said, 'once my son had gone to his father's and I was waiting in my apartment, I heard the footsteps on the stairs and the key turning in the lock and I suddenly became confused as to which of the men I've known in my life was about to walk through the door. It seemed to me in that moment,' she said, 'that I had made too much of the distinctions between these men, when at the time the whole world had appeared to depend on whether I was with one rather than another. I realised that I had believed in them,' she said, 'and in the ecstasy or agony they caused me, but now I could barely recall why and could barely separate them from one another in my mind.'

Sophia's audience at the table were becoming visibly uncomfortable, twitching in their chairs and allowing their eyes to rove, embarrassed, around the room, except for Luís, who sat very still and watched her steadily with an impassive expression.

'Deep down,' she said, 'I felt that these relation-ships lacked the authenticity of my relationship with my ex-husband, and I was always finding fault with the men themselves as a way of explaining this feel-ing: one man didn't speak languages as well as my husband did; another couldn't cook; another wasn't as good at sport. It almost felt,' she said, 'as if it were a contest, and that if these men were inferior to my husband in any way he would win that contest, and I would explain this uncharitable attitude to myself as merely the product of my own fear of him. My hus-band came very close to killing me,' she said, 'without ever laying a finger on me, and I saw now that it was my willingness to be killed that allowed him to get that far, just as it was my belief in one man or another that allowed him to cause me pleasure or pain. But in my apartment, listening to the key turning in the door, it suddenly seemed to me that my husband him-self could be the man about to enter and that finally it would make no difference, because the woman he knew – the woman who had believed in his persona – was no longer there.

'You say,' she said to Luís, 'that you are refusing to tell the story any more, perhaps for some of the same reasons, because you don't believe in the characters or in yourself as a character, or perhaps because stories need cruelty in order for them to work and you have washed your hands of that drama too. But when my son made those comments to me about the photographs, I realised that he had somehow, without my quite noticing, taken the burden of perception from me, which to my mind was inseparable from the burden of living and of telling the story. He showed me in that moment that it was, in fact, separate, and the effect on me was to make me feel an incredible sense of freedom, at the same time as suspecting that by shedding that burden I would have nothing else to live for. You have to live,' she said to Luís, reaching her hand imploringly to him across the table, and he reluctantly reached out his own hand and gave hers a squeeze before withdrawing it. 'No one can take that obligation from you.'

One of the organisers came to the table and said that the bus was now ready to take us back to the hotel. Outside the restaurant, passing through the graffitied concrete lot where the boy was no longer to be seen playing his flute, the Welsh novelist remarked that things had got pretty intense back there.

'I wondered whether Sophia was making a bit of a play for Luís,' he said in a low voice, glancing to either side of him, where the ruined walls of the buildings showed dark voids behind their crumbling edges and the wind sent the weeds growing along the roadside rocking back and forth. 'Actually,' he said, 'I think they'd make quite a good couple.'

I asked him whether he would be attending Sophia's reading, which was scheduled for the afternoon, and he said that unfortunately he wouldn't be able to make it. He was writing a piece about attitudes to the Brexit vote in Wales that had to be delivered by the end of the day. It had been widely observed that the people who lived in the most hopeless poverty and ugliness were those who had voted most overwhelmingly to leave, and nowhere was that truer than his own small country.

'It was a bit of a case of turkeys voting for Christmas,' he said. 'Though obviously I can't say that in print.'

There were housing estates down south, he said, in the post-industrial wastelands, where the men still rode ponies and shot at one another with guns and the women brewed up cauldrons of magic mushrooms in their kitchens: he didn't imagine they spent a lot of time discussing their membership of the EU, if they even knew what it was. In all seriousness it was sad, he added, that the country had come together in what was essentially an act of self-harm, though he himself would luckily be unaffected, since most of his sales revenue came from abroad: ironically, in fact, the more the pound fell against the euro, the better off he was. But it had spoiled the atmosphere even in his own community, where friendly neighbourliness had been replaced by mutual suspicion. He was all for people speaking their minds, but it did make him miss the time when what was beneath the surface had been permitted to stay there. The day after the referendum, he said, he had been visiting his parents in Leicestershire and had stopped for petrol and a cup of coffee in a service station. It was a dismal place, and the man sitting next to him – a great pockmarked tattooed creature – was tucking into a huge plate of fried food and announcing to the whole room that at long last he could be an Englishman eating a full English breakfast in his own country.

'It makes you think democracy wasn't such a good idea after all,' he said.

I said I had assumed his family came from Wales, and he glanced at me with his strange wary smile, showing his narrow yellow teeth.

'I grew up just outside Corby,' he said. 'To be honest it was pretty dull. I keep thinking I'll write about it one day, but there just isn't a lot to say.'

The next morning the wind had dropped and the sagging grey clouds had begun to thin and lift, and by the time the delegates had started to gather in the lobby an intense heat had arrived that seemed to wait behind the veil of cloud, half-threat and half-promise.

Some of them wanted to go to the beach and the organisers were sombrely conferring and looking at their watches. The beach was at least half an hour's walk away, they said: unfortunately it would be impossible to get there and back in time for the next event. Someone asked whether there would be simultaneous translation provided for that event, whose subject was contemporary interpretations of the Bible, and the organisers said that unfortunately in this case they were unable to provide simultaneous translation: this weekend was a big religious festival here, and a lot of their staff had gone home to their families. Also there was the cup final, which they were worried would further deplete audience numbers. They act, a man called Eduardo said to me, as though they are the victims of fate, but in fact these are events that could have been seen from a long way off and avoided. Yet perhaps, he said, it is the very intentness of our own will that causes us to be blind to other realities. A few years ago, he said, some friends of his rented a house in Italy and chose to travel there by car, simply keying the address into their satnav and following its directions, which miraculously took them all the way from Holland – where they lived – down through Europe to this farmhouse in the remotest regions of the hot south. They spent two weeks there, marvelling at their own freedom and autonomy and the ease with which they had made this transition. When the time came to go home and they had packed up the car again, they found that the satnav was for some reason not working. They realised, he said, that they had absolutely no idea where they were – they didn't even know the name of the nearest town – and since they spoke not one word of the language and were in any case in the middle of an unpopulated wilderness, they were forced to drive around and around this savage landscape on dirt roads, trying in increasing panic to find an escape route before they ran out of petrol and food. All that time, he said smiling, when they thought they were free, they were in fact lost without knowing it.

He asked whether I would be attending the Bible talk, which since I wouldn't be able to understand it I would have to treat as a mystical experience in itself, and I said that in fact I was going into the city for the day, as my editor had arranged a few interviews for me to do while I was here. He nodded his head slightly sadly, as though this information represented a disappointment, though to whom it wasn't clear. I had chosen a propitious time for my visit, he said, since it happened to be the brief season when the city's jacaranda trees were in bloom. They were a feature of the landscape there, running in great tall columns along the boulevards and avenues and decorating the many famous squares. Yet it was only for the merest couple of weeks that they burst into flower, producing great ethereal clouds of luminous violet clusters, which moved in the breezes almost in the manner of water or indeed of music, as though the pretty purple flowers were the individual notes that in chorus formed a rippling body of sound. These trees took an extraordinarily long time to grow, he said, and the towering specimens in the city were decades – indeed centuries – old. People sometimes tried to grow them in their own gardens, but unless you were fortunate enough to have inherited one, it was almost impossible to reproduce this spectacle on your own private property. He had many friends – smart, aspirational people of good taste – who had planted a jacaranda tree in their new garden as though this law of nature somehow didn't apply to them and they could make it grow by the force of their will. After a year or two they would become frustrated and complain that it had barely increased even an inch. But it would take twenty, thirty, forty years for one of these trees to grow and yield its beautiful display, he said smiling: when you tell them this fact they are horrified, perhaps because they can't imagine remaining in the same house or indeed the same marriage for so long, and they almost come to hate their jacaranda tree, he said, sometimes even digging it up and replacing it with something else, because it reminds them of the possibility that it is patience and endurance and loyalty – rather than ambition and desire – that bring the ultimate rewards. It is almost a tragedy, he said, that the same people who are capable of wanting the jacaranda tree and understanding its beauty are incapable of nurturing one themselves.

He was acquainted with my editor, he added, since the city was in the end a small world and everyone more or less knew everyone else. In a community as static as theirs, other people's lives were an ongoing drama that kept evolving through different phases of existence, like a long-running soap opera; occasionally a new character would come in, but the core cast remained the same. Paola was a good woman, he said, though one of those to whom something is always happening and who always somehow manages to come out of it stronger. In this country, for a woman to survive the numerous attempts to crush her, he said, she has to live like a hero, always getting up again and always, ultimately, alone.

On the television in front of the deserted sofas, a huge crowd was gathered around a church, holding aloft wreaths of flowers and candles while a man in ecclesiastical costume addressed them through a microphone. A little girl with an enormous blue satin bow in her hair and a matching elaborately frilled dress stood staring at the screen while her parents called to her from inside the open lifts.

'Our embarrassing secret,' Eduardo said, rolling his eyes at the religious spectacle on the television. 'You can possibly cope with thinking half the country is mad, but then tomorrow, with the football, it becomes clear the other half is mad too.'

The other delegates were gathering on the tarmac beyond the plate-glass windows, waiting to be taken to the next event. We passed out through the doors and into the car park, where he looked doubtfully at the sky.

'You have seen us in strange weather,' he said. 'But I think it's about to improve.'

Hammering sun, he added, was the norm at this time of year: these melancholy interludes of grey confusion were rare and yet nonetheless had the most dispiriting effect, as though they represented the temporary absence of authority. Dictatorial as it was, the sun was at least consistent: in England you are used to the sky weeping on you, he said, but here we take these things personally, like children take their parents' moods personally and assume they are to blame. Perhaps it follows, he said, that people who live in the sun don't take responsibility for their own happiness. According to his son, the unseasonal weather had at least yielded some excellent surf conditions, which undoubtedly meant that he and his friends would pack up and move to the beach for a few days, with no more ambition than a colony of seals, he said, who go where the forces of nature direct them. My children live in only two dimensions, he said, like the character Tintin, whose adventures are made possible by occurring in a world that is fixed and that can be represented by a cartoonist's pen, where for me it is people and their thoughts that have been the true reality. I treated my children with only kindness, he said, and the result is that they have none of the anxieties I had at their age and also none of the ideas and visions by which I believed the world could be transformed and which turned even the smallest things into elements of a great drama, so that everything always seemed to be in a state of flux. For them the world is fixed, as I say, and they are willing to take their piece of it, but in the end it will be a much smaller piece, he said, than that which I have taken myself, despite the fact that I have apparently devoted myself to the life of the mind. I have more than they will probably ever have, he said smiling, yet I appear to them as a tortured soul: they are always giving me advice designed to make me happier and more relaxed, and it is good advice, he said, but they don't seem to realise that if I took it the drama would be over and the world would have less interest for me. The other day, he said, my son and I were talking about politics, and he observed that in the current situation the possibility of destruction seemed genuinely to be upon us, to the extent that he couldn't see what move on the chess board would get us out of this corner. I replied that this was something all of us had felt in our turn, as we passed into adulthood and recognised the role of outside events in shaping history and their capacity to interfere in and change our lives, which until now had remained in the hermetic state of childhood. He said something which very much surprised me, which was that in any case he felt the destruction had by now been earned in full by humanity, and that even if it meant the lives of his generation weren't allowed to run their full course, he believed it would be for the best. Every time he thought of the future, his son said, he had to remind himself that this sense of his own story was just an illusion, because not enough was left any more for another story: enough time, enough material, enough authenticity. Everything has been used up, he said, except I suppose, Eduardo added, the waves, which continue to pound on the shore and will still be pounding when we're gone.

The bus had arrived and the queue of delegates was shuffling forwards through the open doors. Eduardo held out his hand. The sun suddenly broke through the cloud and surged hot and fierce across our faces and the tarmac of the car park and the glinting metal of the bus.

'I suspect that you are running away,' he said, his eyes screwed up either with puzzlement or because of the heavy glare. 'I hope you make good use of your freedom.'

The hotel where Paola had asked me to meet her was as plush as the one from which I'd come had been bleak. The walls of the vast lobby were panelled with dark wood and leather, and an air of mystery had been created by the use of columns and dim lighting and lowered sections of ceiling, so although the people inside remained visible, it encouraged them to feel concealed. The reception desk, an enormous dark plinth in a sunken hall staffed by a row of uniformed attendants, gave such an impression of grandiose finality that it was as if, Paola said, this was where the wheat was being separated from the chaff. She sat perched on a leather footstool in a silvery tunic and thin gold sandals, tapping speedily at the screen of her phone and shooting enquiring looks around the lobby while her assistant, a large soft girl with a sweetly placid expression, sat on a sofa nearby. The hotel, Paola said, laid claim to literary associations that were more or less spurious, since they consisted entirely of the fact that a bookshop had once stood on this site which was demolished to make way for the new building. Nonetheless the theme had been conserved in the hotel's insignia – a motif of famous signatures written in faded ink – and in the severe splendour of its decor, though in their haste to re-create the ambiance of a library they had somehow, she said, forgotten to supply any books, except for the wallpaper made from a photograph of worn leather spines that had been used for the inside of the lifts. But we should be grateful, she said, that they took such a serious attitude to literature, because even if this place was entirely unrepresentative of writers and their lives, it was ideal for conducting interviews and in summer was one of the coolest and quietest spots in the city.

The first journalist would be arriving at any moment, she added, and there would be a filmed interview later, on behalf of the last remaining arts programme on national television. Only a handful of writers were invited to participate in this programme, she went on, so she was happy I was one of them, because opportunities to promote books were harder and harder to come by. The format was very straightforward and the whole thing would probably only take fifteen minutes, since the programme had had its running time cut in half last year. It was unclear precisely why this had happened, she added, except that everything to do with literature always seemed to be shrinking, as though the world of books was governed by a principle of entropy while everything else proliferated and expanded. The newspapers now gave half the space to reviews that they had ten years ago and bookshops were forever closing down, and with the arrival of the e-reader there had even been doomsayers predicting the book as a physical entity might cease to exist entirely. Like the Siberian tiger, she said, we are always being threatened with extinction, as though novels likewise had once been fierce and were now fragile and defenceless. Somewhere along the line, she said, we have failed to promote our product, perhaps because the people who work in the literary world are those who secretly believe their interest in literature is a weakness, a kind of debility that marks them out from everyone else. We publishers, she said, proceed on the assumption that no one cares about books, whereas the makers of cornflakes convince everyone that the world needs cornflakes like it needs the sun to rise in the morning.

Her eyes had been busily scanning the lobby and they suddenly lit up at the sight of a man coming through the big smoked-glass doors. She leapt off her stool and went to meet him, while her assistant asked me if I wanted any coffee before things got started. There would probably be some free time between the interviews, she said, but you could never be sure:

sometimes they went on for much longer than they were supposed to. Some writers perhaps had more to say than others did, she said doubtfully, or perhaps they just enjoyed talking more. I asked her how long she had worked in publishing and she said she had only had this job for a couple of months. Before that she had worked for one of the national airlines. This was a better job, she said, because the hours were more sociable and it meant she could spend more time with her children. Her children were very small, she said, but she had got into the habit of asking each of the writers she met to sign a copy of their book with a dedication for them. She put the books on a special shelf at home, because although the children were too young to read them now, she liked the idea of them finding a shelf with all these books dedicated to them in the future. Perhaps, she said, if there was time, she could trouble me to sign one of mine for them later.

The journalist had sat down on a nearby sofa and was leafing through his notes. He stood up to shake my hand, wearing an expression of great serious-ness: he was very tall and entirely bald and his thick-framed glasses were so large they seemed designed to magnify his role as interrogator at the same time as offering the hope that he might not be seen. His skin was extremely pale and his large hairless head had a somewhat glimmering, preternatural appearance in the dim room. The assistant offered him water, which he accepted with raised eyebrows, as though the offer had surprised him. Beside him on the table was a pile of books, the pages bristling with Post-it notes. He hoped I wasn't finding it too hot in the city, he said: he himself couldn't bear this time of year, since unlike most of his countrymen he had a very fair skin that suffered badly in the sun. He preferred the English climate, where even a summer's day had a caressing silkiness to it and the trees, to quote from Tennyson, laid their dark arms across the lawn, though of course the English themselves came here in their hordes – he grimaced with his rather plump pale mouth – to lie roasting on the beaches. He had wondered, he added, whether out of tact or courtesy or just plain shame they might desist from this habit in the light of their recent rejection of European membership, but there was no sign that this was the case.

'There they sit,' he said, folding his arms and looking theatrically around himself with defiant bullishness, in imitation of these interlopers, 'entrenched in the resorts and watering holes, unable to converse in any but their native tongue nor even to comprehend the implications of their own boorish stupidity. Like great big babies,' he said, somewhat resembling an over-sized baby himself, 'who have managed to derail the whole family because no one made the effort to bring them up properly. At one time I had a love affair with England,' he added, resuming his normal demeanour. 'I loved its poetry and its irony – I loved it so much I cursed the fact I hadn't been born an Englishman. But now,' he said, 'I feel lucky not to be one.'

The changing perspectives of identity, he went on, was a subject he sensed I had given some consideration to: was it not the case that one could believe oneself to be disadvantaged by things that later were proved to be assets, and conversely – and perhaps more commonly – that there were people who remained convinced they were the favourites of the gods until life taught them otherwise? As a scholarly boy with no sporting ability, for instance, he had regarded himself as seriously disabled until it was revealed that a good brain was worth far more than the knack of catching a ball. A friend of his had a phrase that always amused him: life, this friend said, was the revenge of the nerds, and this charming notion – that it was the bookish laughing stocks who ended up with the power – acquired certain nuances when one applied it to writers, for whom the question of power generally remained unresolved. A writer was only given power by the act of someone reading their book: this was perhaps why so many writers became obsessed with having their books made into films, since it dispensed with the arduous part of that transaction. In the case of the English, their power was a memory, and the spectacle of them attempting to exercise it was as ridiculous as that of a dog dreaming it is chasing a rabbit.

It was his practice to read the entirety of an author's oeuvre, he added, seeing me glance at the pile of books, and not just the latest one, as so many of his colleagues did. He had often been surprised by how many authors seemed to feel that this constituted an investigation into their past life, as though the books had no existence in the public realm and he had somehow caught them out. On one occasion, an author was unable to remember anything at all about a book he had written a few years earlier; on another, a female novelist had admitted that she liked only one of the many books she'd written – books that her readers still bought and presumably read – and felt the others to be pretty much worthless. Still others – and this was admittedly far more common – seemed to value their work on the basis of the rewards and recognition it had received, and to have adopted the world's assessment of their own importance; but only, he added, adjusting his glasses, if that assessment was positive. What surprised him was that these writers seemed, when they embarked on their career, to have had no particular plan, and to have written books much as other people got up and went to work in the morning. It was, in other words, simply their job, and was as provisional and exposed to the possibility of boredom and mundanity as any other job: they didn't know what the future would bring, though they subscribed to the same vague belief in progress as everyone else, and they were likewise liable to make much of their successes while blaming their failures on other people's ignorance, as well as on luck, which was the chief means by which they believed that certain others among their contemporaries had got ahead.

'I admit it has been something of a disappointment to me to make these discoveries,' he said, 'because I revere literary art, and though I accept that an early novel even by a great master might lack the depth and complexity of a later work, I don't especially want to feel that by reading an author's oeuvre I am merely watching them stumbling through life, only marginally less blindfolded than everyone else.'

He had always been compelled by provocative and difficult writing, he went on, because this at least proved the author had had the wit to unshackle himself from convention, but he had found that in works of extreme negativity – the writings of Thomas Bernhard were an example he had been considering lately – one nonetheless eventually hit an impasse. A work of art could not, ultimately, be negative: its material existence, its status as an object, could not help but be positive, a gain, an addition to the sum of what was. The self-destructive novel, like the self-destructive person, was something from which in the end you remained helplessly separated, forced to watch a spectacle – the soul turning on itself – in which you were powerless to intervene. Great art was very often brought to the service of this self-immolation, as great intelligence and sensitivity often characterised those who found the world an impossible place to live in; yet the spectre of madness was so discomfiting that it made surrender to the writing unfeasible; one stayed on one's guard, as a child might stay on its guard against a mad parent, knowing itself ultimately alone. Negative literature, he had noticed, got much of its power through the fearless use of honesty: a person with no interest in living and hence no investment in the future can afford to be honest, he said, and the same dubious privilege was extended to the negative writer. Yet their honesty, as he had said, was of an unpalatable kind: in a sense it went to waste, perhaps because no one cared for the honesty of someone who was jumping the ship the rest of us were stuck on. The real honesty, of course, was that of the person who remained on board and endeavoured to tell the truth about it, or so we were led to believe. If I agreed that literature was a form that took its life-blood from social and material constructs, the writer could do no more than stay within those constructs, buried in bourgeois life – as he had recently read it described somewhere – like a tick in an animal's fur.

He paused, searching for something in his notes, while I observed the extraordinary pallor and tenderness of his hairless head bent over the pages. Presently he looked up again, fixing me in the giant orbs of his glasses. The question he wished to discuss with me, he said, was the question of whether I believed there was a third kind of honesty, beyond that of the person who leaves and that of the person who stays; an honesty to which no moral bias could be ascribed, that is interested neither in debunking nor in reforming, that has no compass of its own and can describe evil as dispassionately as virtue without erring on the side of one or the other, that is as pure and reflective as water or glass. He believed certain French writers had become interested in this question, he said – Georges Bataille came to mind as an example – but to him they went no further than positing honesty as amoral, in other words as refusing to differentiate between good and bad and offering no judgement on one or the other. His question was more, in a sense, old-fashioned: could a spiritual value be attached to the mirror itself, so that by passing dispassionately through evil it proved its own virtue, its own incorruptibility? Did I not, in the end, thirst for that proof, to the extent that I might consider evil as a subject?

For the sake of fairness he ought perhaps to tell me, he added, that he was known in this city as a maker and breaker of reputations: a bad review from him could kill a book, and so one consequence of his own honesty was that he had many enemies, which meant that when he brought out a book of his own – he had so far produced three volumes of poetry – the knives, as they say, were out. These attacks had resulted in his work not gaining the recognition it might otherwise have received: he had applied for numerous academic fellowships in the States, as well as for literary posts in this country, and had been unsuccessful, yet his power as a critic remained undiminished; indeed, if anything it was constantly increasing, to the extent that he was acquiring an international reputation. Friends of his had advised him that if he wanted to make it as a creative writer, he should stop savaging other people's work, but you might as well ask a bird not to fly or a cat not to hunt; and besides, what would his poetry be worth if he wrote it while living in the same zoo as all the other denatured animals, safe but not free? And that was without even mentioning the moral duty of the critic to correct the tendency of culture likewise to err towards safety and medio-crity, a responsibility you couldn't measure in dinner invitations.

What he couldn't tolerate above all else, he went

on, was the triumph of the second-rate, the dishonest, the ignorant: the fact that this triumph occurred
with monotonous regularity was one of life's mysteries, and he was well aware that in pitting himself against it he ran the risk of succumbing to the
same despair that made the literature of negativity so
impotent. Too much time among the Pharisees and
not enough with the devil himself: this was how, he
said, the question of evil had come to interest him.
He was only twenty-six – he was aware, he said, that
he looked much older – and when he had alluded
to those writers who seemed to have no overarch-
ing plan and who claimed not even to know what
was going to happen in the book they were currently
writing, as though their work were the result not of
careful thought or artistic competence or merely hard
work, but of divine inspiration or worse, imagination,
he was not describing himself. He wouldn't start a
piece of writing without knowing precisely where it
was going to lead any more than he would leave his
house without knowing what his destination was or
without his keys and wallet. Such claims were the
bane of our culture, he said, because they imputed
a kind of feeble-mindedness to the arts, where men
and women in other fields were proud of their self-
discipline and competence. He expected, he said,
that I would agree with this assessment, since he had

185

deduced from my work that if I had an imagination I had the sense to keep it well concealed.

'And there is no better hiding place,' he said, 'than somewhere as close as possible to the truth, something all good liars know.'

He was looking up at something over my shoulder and I turned to see the assistant standing there. She was very sorry, she said, but the interview had now run its allotted course, and since the next interview was for television and involved precise timings, we would have to bring things to a conclusion. The journalist immediately began to remonstrate with her and a lengthy exchange ensued, in which he spoke very quickly and forcefully and she replied very slowly, repeating certain phrases and nodding her head with sympathetic regret, until finally he began irritably to pack his books and notes back into his briefcase. Her training with the airline, she said, as she led me away towards the lifts, had come in handy more times than she might have expected in this job. She had to admit this journalist was one of her trickier customers, and his interviews nearly always ended with the same argument, since he seemed to take such a long time to get round to asking a question and when he did, discovered that he himself had the best answer for it. She mildly rolled her eyes and pressed the button to call the lift. In fact she had gone to the same school as him, she added, and often saw him at family occasions, but whenever they met through work he pretended not to know her. At home he is very polite and nice, she said wistfully, as well as being the only one prepared to talk to the grandmothers, who will listen to him for hours on end.

The hotel had given permission for a temporary studio to be set up in the basement, she said as the lift went down, and though it didn't look quite as professional as their usual set, the illusion was actually quite convincing. We emerged into a large, low-ceilinged space where several people were absorbed in adjusting wires and lights amid piles of camera equipment. In the far corner, surrounded by bare concrete walls and packing cases, a small segment of a room had been re-created, with tall bookshelves and pictures and a threadbare Persian rug on which two antique chairs had been placed at a conversational angle. A number of very bright lights were trained on it, giving it the appearance of a golden book-lined island, with the men working in a kind of purgatorial gloom just beyond its shores. A slender woman with a wide pale face elaborately made up for the camera approached us and held out her hand. She wore a high-necked blouse with long buttoned sleeves and her long thick pale-gold hair was drawn smoothly back in a ponytail, like a studious princess with the book-lined island as her home. She would be conducting the interview, she said in English, and once the men had sorted out a small problem with the sound equipment we could probably get started straight away. She turned and said something to the assistant and the two of them talked back and forth for a while, sometimes laughing and laying a hand on one another's arm, while the men silently and absorbedly worked at the equipment, plugging and unplugging long trailing wires and rummaging in the big black camera cases that lay open around them on the floor. Presently the interviewer indicated that they wanted us to take our places, and we went and sat on the antique chairs among the bookshelves, where the bright light caused everything around it to fall into half-darkness, so that the cameramen became obscure figures moving through the murky shadow. A man who was evidently the director stood just at the edge of the light, issuing instructions to the interviewer while she slowly nodded her head, occasionally looking at me out of the corner of her painted eye and giving me a complicit smile.

The technicians were asking us to talk, she said to me, so that they could adjust the sound levels and work out what the problem was. They had told us to just talk about what we had for breakfast today, she said, though there were probably more interesting things we could discuss. She was hoping our conversation would focus on the problem of recognition for female writers and artists: perhaps I had some thoughts on that subject I could share with her, so that she could make sure to ask the right questions in the interview. The topic probably wasn't new to me, but it might well never have occurred to their viewers that the same inequalities that beset the home and the workplace could dictate what was presented to them as art, so she saw no reason not to give the nail another bang on the head. And it was of course true, she added, that few notable women were ever really recognised, or at least not until they had been judged to be no longer a public danger by having become old or ugly or dead. The artist Louise Bourgeois, for example, was suddenly all the rage in her last years and finally allowed to come out of the closet and be seen, when her male counterparts had been on the public stage all along, entertaining people with their grandiose and self-destructive behaviour. Yet if one looked at the work of Louise Bourgeois, one saw that it concerned the private history of the female body, its suppression and exploitation and transmogrifications, its terrible malleability as a form and its capacity to create other forms. It was tempting to consider, she said, that Bourgeois's talent relied on the anonymity of her experiences; in other words, that had she been recognised as a younger artist, she might not have had cause to dwell on the ignominious mysteries of her life as a woman, and instead would have been partying and posing for the front covers of magazines along with the rest of them. There are a number of works, she said, executed when Bourgeois was the mother of small children, in which she portrays herself as a spider, and what is interesting about these works is not just what they convey about the condition of motherhood – in distinct contrast, she said, to the perennial male vision of the ecstatically fulfilled madonna – but also the fact that they appear to be children's drawings drawn in a child's hand. It is hard to think, she said, of a better example of female invisibility than these drawings, in which the artist herself has disappeared and exists only as the benign monster of her child's perception. Plenty of female practitioners of the arts, she said, have more or less ignored their femininity, and it might be argued that these women have found recognition easier to come by, perhaps because they draw a veil over subjects that male intellectuals find distasteful, or perhaps simply because they have chosen not to fulfil their own biological destiny and therefore have had more time to concentrate on their work. It is understandable, she said, that a woman of talent might resent being fated to the feminine subject and might seek freedom by engaging with the world on other terms; yet the image of Bourgeois's spider, she said, seems almost to reproach the woman who has run away from these themes and left the rest of us stuck, as it were, in our webs.

She paused for a moment to look enquiringly towards the camera lights, beyond which the men were gathered in shadowy consultation, their arms full of cables. The director shook his head and she raised a perfectly drawn eyebrow and then slowly returned her gaze to me.

I remember, she continued, as a young girl, the realisation dawning on me that certain things had been decided for me before I had even begun to live, and that I had already been dealt the losing hand while my brother had been given the winning cards. It would be a mistake, I saw, to treat this injustice as though it were normal, as all my friends seemed prepared to do; and it was not so very hard to get the better of that situation, she said, because the boy that is handed all the cards is perhaps also very slightly complacent, as well as having a big question mark in the form of the thing between his legs, which he must work out what to do with. These boys, she said, had the most ridiculous attitudes towards women, which they were busy learning from the examples their parents had given them, and I saw the way that my female friends defended themselves against those attitudes, by making themselves as perfect and as inoffensive as they could. Yet the ones who didn't defend themselves were just as bad, because by refusing to conform to these standards of perfection they were in a sense disqualifying themselves and distancing themselves from the whole subject. But I quickly came to see, she said, that in fact there was nothing worse than to be an average white male of average talents and intelligence: even the most oppressed housewife, she said, is closer to the drama and poetry of life than he is, because as Louise Bourgeois shows us she is capable at least of holding more than one perspective. And it was true, she said, that a number of girls were achieving academic success and cultivating professional ambitions, to the extent that people had begun to feel sorry for these average boys and to worry that their feelings were being hurt. Yet if you looked only a little way ahead, she said, you could see that the girls' ambitions led nowhere, like the roads you often find yourself on in this country, that start off new and wide and smooth and then simply stop in the middle of nowhere, because the government ran out of money to finish building them.

She paused again and glanced over at the director, who gave her a thumbs-down, and gestured for her to continue talking. She carefully tucked a lock of her straight, pale-yellow hair behind her ear and then folded her hands in her lap.

At around this time, she said, I began to discover

the worlds of literature and art and I found there much of the information I needed, information my mother had neglected to pass on to me, perhaps in the hope that I would somehow make my way through this minefield in ignorance unscathed and that if she alerted me to the dangers I might take fright and make a misstep. I made sure to work hard, she said, and to achieve the highest results, but no matter how hard I worked there was always a boy there, level with me, who appeared to be less out of breath and to be taking things in his stride; and so I cultivated the art, she said, of nonchalance, and gave every impression of being less well-prepared than I was, until one day I found that this impression had become a reality, and that I achieved even more by leaving a few things to chance and by taking a leap of faith, such as the child takes when the training wheels come off the bicycle and it finds itself cycling unsupported for the first time. I also enjoyed the attentions of men, she said, while making sure never to commit myself to any one man or to ask for commitment in return, because I understood that this was a trap and that I could still enjoy all the benefits of a relationship without falling into it. At a certain point it struck me that I could even have a child, she said, without necessarily compromising myself in the usual ways. But I didn't really want a child, she said, despite the fact that my friends were having them and could talk of little else, because it seemed to me that there were so many children, she said, and that if I could manage without one then I ought at least to try. It did not seem like enough, she said, simply to pass the baton to the next runner, in the hope that she would win the race for me.

The job that I do, she said, gazing at me steadily with her clear, almond-shaped pale-blue eyes, is in many respects a superficial one, since it involves being looked at, and part of the reason I was given it was because of my ability to manipulate my appearance. I have a male counterpart on the show, she said, and he is not required to look attractive, but I am not in the slightest bit interested in that example of inequality. What I am interested in is power, she said, and the power of beauty is a useful weapon that too often women disparage or misuse. My background is principally in the visual rather than the literary arts, she said, because that is where these politics are decided and where the battles of life are mainly fought and it is also, she said, where the nature of male superiority is at its most exposed. For a while, at university, I sat as a life model for the art students, she said, partly to make money and partly to get this subject of the female body out into the open, because it almost seemed to me that even by clothing myself I was inviting the mystery to take root there under my clothes, and to weave the web of subjection in which later I might become trapped. I myself was taking art history, she said, and for my thesis I studied the work of the British artist Joan Eardley, whose position struck me as an example of the tragedy of female authority, though in a very different way from that of Louise Bourgeois or indeed of the poet Sylvia Plath, who remains as a warning to us all of the price to be paid for the fulfilment of one's biological destiny. Joan Eardley hid herself away on a tiny island off the coast of Scotland, she said, where she documented the savageries of nature, of the cliffs and the tempestuous sea and the sky, always seeming to be standing on the edge of some unspeakable violence or turbulence, she said, as though she were trying to locate the edge of the world itself. She spent a certain amount of time also in the city of Glasgow, where she drew and painted the street children, whose poverty and depressing cheerfulness she was unable to observe entirely without sentiment: she drew them obsessively and also it seems involved herself in their lives, rather as Degas haunted the world of his ballet dancers, she said, with the difference that Joan Eardley was not a man and so her vision appears disturbing and strange rather than familiar and legitimate. Also on her visits to the Glasgow slums she painted certain men, people she encountered on the streets or in the boarding houses, and again treated these subjects as some of the famous male artists have. There is a painting by Eardley, she said, of a male nude asleep on a bed: he is lying on his side, his grey, bony, undernourished body entirely revealed, in a room that is also unrelievedly grey, and the bed is as narrow and comfortless as a coffin. This painting, she said, is unlike anything else I have seen painted by a woman, and partly because of its large size it seems to take the bleakest possible view of life, so that it almost succeeds in refuting the whole history of men paint-ing women in such poses. The pathos of that sleeping body, she said, its lack of any promise or possibility, is entirely shocking, and indeed the painting caused a scandal at the time, for the resemblance between this man and the victims of the concentration camps with whose images the world had become familiar a few years earlier. Yet despite that scandal – which re-sulted, bizarrely, she said, in a number of men turning up at Eardley's door and offering themselves as her next nude model – Eardley's oeuvre remains unrecog-nised and her life, which as far as I can ascertain was without sex and was certainly childless and solitary, ended in agonising illness at the age of forty-two. It was a life without illusion, she said, and it seems to me that it remains impossible for a woman to live without illusion, because the world will simply snuff her out.

In my own case, she said, I have fought to occupy

a position where I can perhaps right some of these wrongs and can adjust the terms of the debate to an extent by promoting the work of women I find interesting. But increasingly, she said, this position feels like I am standing on a small rock in the ocean that is getting even smaller by the minute as the water rises. There has been no territory marked out, she said, and so there is no place where I can take a step and find myself still on dry land. It perhaps remains the case, she said, that for a woman to have a territory she must live as Bourgeois's spider, unless she is prepared to camp on male territory and abide by its terms. There are as yet only two roles, she said, that of model and that of artist and the alternative, she said, as the men moving through the gloom began shaking their heads at one another and the director threw up his hands in a gesture of despair, is to disappear into some belief or philosophy and find a shelter that way. She cocked her head, listening while the director spoke to her, and then turned to me with her slender, elegant eyebrows disparagingly raised.

'It seems extraordinary,' she said, 'that all these men together can't fix the problem, but they say they will have to take the equipment back to the studio to repair it. It is very disappointing,' she said, rising from her chair and beginning to disentangle the microphone cord from her clothing, 'and considering the subject of our conversation, more than a little ironic.'

The third interview, the assistant said on our way back upstairs, would be the last one, and she hoped it was more successful than the other two had been. She believed Paola had booked a restaurant afterwards for lunch, so hopefully I would have the opportunity to relax before returning to the conference. We emerged into the lobby, where Paola was sitting on her stool talking on the phone. She waved and rolled her eyes and the assistant led me back to the sofa where the first interview had occurred and where a man was waiting, though in fact when we got closer I saw that he was hardly more than a boy. He sat lightly on the edge of his seat, dressed in a white T-shirt and a faded pair of jeans and dangling a baseball cap loosely from his fingers, a mildly anxious expression of innocence on his face, like that of a young saint in a religious painting. He sprang up to shake my hand and then waited politely for me to sit down before returning to his place. His brown hair fell in ringlets around his guileless, almost feminine features, and his darker brown eyes were fixed on mine with childlike earnestness.

'I wonder,' he said eventually, 'if you have ever thought of what it would be like to live in the sun. I got the idea from your book,' he added. 'One of the characters talks about how he has lived his whole life in the rain and the cold, and how being in the sun has

198

changed his character. I wondered if it might be the same for you.'

I said it probably wasn't worth thinking about, since living in the sun wasn't something I planned to do.

'But why not?' he said.

We sat and looked at one another.

'I've thought about it,' he said, 'and I believe it would be the right thing for you to do.'

I asked him where he suggested I should live.

'Here,' he said simply. 'You would be very happy. No one would trouble you. People would be very kind to you. You wouldn't even have to learn the language,' he said, 'because everyone can speak English and they accept that that is the way things are. We would look after you,' he said, 'and everything would be easier. You wouldn't need to suffer any more. You could find a cottage on the coast, by the sea. You would be warm and your skin would turn brown. I've thought about it,' he repeated, 'and I don't see any disadvantages.'

In the dim distances of the lobby people stood or sat or moved around, visible but at an unbreachable distance, as though they were under water. There was a constant low murmur of voices from which no individual word could be distinguished. Sometimes a group moved away and was replaced by another group, and when people came and went with their suitcases through the smoked-glass doors the extraordinary reality of the hot, bright, motionless street outside could momentarily be seen.

I said I wasn't sure it mattered where people lived or how, since their individual nature would create its own circumstances: it was a risky kind of presumption, I said, to rewrite your own fate by changing its setting; when it happened to people against their will, the loss of the known world – whatever its features – was catastrophic. My son once admitted to me, I said, that when he was younger he desperately wished he could belong to a different family, such as the family of a friend of his with whom at a certain period he spent a lot of his time. This family was big and noisy and easy-going, and there was always room for him at the table, where huge comforting meals were served and where everything was discussed but nothing examined, so that there was no danger of passing through the mirror, as he had put it, into the state of painful self-awareness where human fictions lose their credibility.

This was the state into which he felt our own family life had been forced, I said, and for a while he had done everything he could to hold on to those fictions, insisting on the old routines and the old traditions, even though what they represented was no longer there. In the end, I said, he gave up and began to absent himself more and more, spending all his time with this other family, as I had said, and refusing to take any of his meals at home, because even sitting around the table, he later admitted, made him feel overwhelmed by sadness and anger at what had been lost. But later, I said, a time came when he was no longer always at the house of this other family, to the extent that the parents began to ask after him and to invite him to family occasions, so that he worried that he had upset or offended them by coming less often. The truth was that he no longer wanted to go there, because the same things that a year or two earlier he had found warm and consoling he now found oppressive and annoying: those mealtimes were a yoke, he now saw, by which the parents sought to bind their children to them and to perpetuate, as he saw it, the family myth; his friend's every movement was subjected to paren- tal scrutiny and his choices and attitudes to parental judgement, and it was this last element – judgement – that my son found most repellent and that drove him away from their door, lest he be subjected to it too. In their invitations for him to return he began to see that the history of his presence there had not been as one-sided as he had thought: in his need for the con- solation they offered he had failed to see that they needed him too, as the witness to – and perhaps even the proof of – their family happiness. He even wondered, bitterly, whether they had enjoyed the spectacle of his misery, because it affirmed the superiority of their own way of life; but in the end, I said, he drew back from that harsh assessment and began to accept their invitations again, not always but often enough for the sake of courtesy. He recognised that in taking their comfort he had created a responsibility towards them; and this realisation, I said, had caused him to consider the true nature of freedom. He understood that he had given some of his freedom away, through a desire to avoid or alleviate his own suffering, and while it didn't seem exactly an unfair exchange, I believed he wouldn't do it again quite so easily.

The journalist had listened to all of this with the same expression of patient innocence on his face.

'But why is it so bad to depend on people?' he said. 'Not everyone is cruel. Perhaps,' he said, 'you have just been unlucky.'

There was a word in his language, I said, that was hard to translate but that could be summed up as a feeling of homesickness even when you are at home, in other words as a sorrow that has no cause. This feeling was perhaps what had once driven his people to roam the world, seeking the home that would cure them of it. It may be the case that to find that home is to end one's quest, I said, but it is with the feeling of displacement itself that the true intimacy develops and that constitutes, as it were, the story. Whatever kind of affliction it is, I said, its nature is that of the compass, and the owner of such a compass puts all his faith in it and goes where it tells him to go, despite appearances telling him the opposite. It is impossible for such a person to attain serenity, I said, and he might spend his whole life marvelling at that quality in others or failing to understand it, and perhaps the best he can hope for is to give a good imitation of it, as certain addicts accept that while they will never be free of their impulses they can live alongside them without acting on them. What such a person cannot tolerate, I said, is the suggestion that his experiences have not arisen out of universal conditions but instead can be blamed on particular or exceptional circumstances, and that what he was treating as truth was in fact no more than personal fortune; any more than the addict, I said, ought to believe that he can regain his innocence of things of which he already has a fatal knowledge.

'Where is he now,' the journalist said, 'the son you talked about?'

I said that he had chosen to go and live with his father for a while, and although I couldn't be said to be happy without him, I hoped he would find what he was looking for.

'But why did you let him go?' he said.

If I had given my children freedom, I said, I couldn't start dictating its terms.

He nodded his head in mournful acquiescence.

'All the same,' he said, 'at a certain point you also are free to choose whether to live in the rain or to live in the sun. We would take good care of you,' he repeated. 'If you didn't want to see anybody, you wouldn't have to. But the people here would appreciate you. I still believe that you have been unlucky,' he said, 'and that if you had lived in this country your experiences would have been different. The character in your book,' he said, 'notices that the dampness that has been inside him his whole life is beginning to dry out and that this might be an opportunity to live for a second time. But he can't, because he has a family back at home and his children are still young. And besides, his national identity is the part of his character from which he believes his success has come. If he didn't have it, he would be the same as everyone else and would have to compete with them on the same terms, and in his heart he knows he doesn't have the talent to win. But you,' he said to me, 'don't belong anywhere, and so you are free to go wherever you choose.'

The assistant approached shyly and said that it was time for the interview to end and for Paola and me to leave for the restaurant. Also, she wondered whether it would bother me too much to sign two of my books for her children, as she had mentioned earlier. She took the books out of a supermarket carrier bag and placed a pen carefully on top of them and held them out to me. I signed the books, the assistant spelling out each of the children's names for me. The third interviewer rose to leave while Paola, who was still sitting on her stool and talking on her phone, pointed at the phone and then held her finger in the air. Shortly afterwards she flung it in her bag and leapt off the stool and came to join us. The assistant told her about the morning's events and she listened while retrieving her phone from her bag again and tapping something rapidly on the screen. Then she looked at her watch and turned to me. She had booked a restaurant in the old part of town, she said: my translator, a woman called Felícia, would be meeting us there. If I preferred, she said, we could take a taxi, or if I didn't mind the heat we could walk, since there was just about enough time.

'It would be good to walk, no?' she said, her small button-like eyes bright with expectation.

After the sepulchral cool and dimness of the lobby, the heat outside on the pavement was momentarily shocking. A pallor of dust hung in the dry throbbing air beneath the fierce blue of the sky. The street was deserted, apart from a group of office workers who stood across the road in the rectangle of the building's shade, smoking and talking. One or two cats lay stretched out on their sides in the dark spaces beneath parked cars. The noise of distant traffic and of machinery from a building site somewhere nearby droned steadily in the background. We set off along the pavement, Paola moving with surprising rapidity despite her diminutive stature and the thin gold sandals she wore on her feet. She was somewhere in her fifties, but her neat mischievous face with its shining eyes was almost childlike. Her clothes were made of a light, flowing material in which her small, solid, vigorous body strode out freely and she swung her arms, her fine brown hair flying behind her.

'I am a great walker,' she said. 'Here I walk everywhere. It gives me such pleasure,' she said, 'to see people trapped in their cars while I am free.' The capital, as I must know, was famous for the steepness of its terrain. 'Either I am going up or I am going down,' she said. 'Never in the middle.'

She used to have a car, but she drove it so rarely that she was always forgetting where she'd last parked it. Then, one day when she needed it, she found that someone had crashed into it.

'I am perhaps the only person,' she said, 'who could write off their car without even sitting in it. It was completely destroyed,' she said, 'so I just left it there and walked away.'

206

The suburb where I was staying seemed a long way from here, she said, but actually was no more than half an hour on foot, if you knew which way to go: it was only because of the peculiarities of the road system and the lack of public transport that it seemed much further. Yet it felt so cut off out there that she had heard numerous stories over the years – some of them quite entertaining – of authors absconding or attempting to escape.

'But in fact,' she said, 'you have been quite close to civilisation all along.'

A lot of people were incapacitated by the city's heat, she added, even those who had lived here all their lives, but she herself had learned the art of conserving her energy and not wasting it battling against forces over which she had no control. When her son was small, for example, she would rise early so that he would always find her fully dressed in the kitchen, making breakfast and ready for the day: she would take him to nursery, talking cheerfully all the way, and when she had dropped him off would promptly return home, remove all her clothes again and get straight back into bed to sleep. Her prodigious walking was offset by periods in which she would often remain entirely stationary for literally hours at a time, like a reptile, she said, who doesn't even use the energy it takes to blink. She had lived here for thirty-five years, she said, in answer to my question, having spent her childhood in the remote north of the country.

'There,' she said, 'everything is water. The sky is always heavy and the rivers are full and everywhere there is the sound of dripping and trickling and pouring, so that when you are there you almost become mesmerised.'

Recently, she had gone back and spent a few weeks at home because her mother had been ill.

'It was so strange to find myself in that watery environment again,' she said, 'with the sound of the rain falling and the rivers rushing downhill towards the sea, and the damp grass everywhere and the heavy, dripping trees. After a while I began to remember things I had completely forgotten,' she said, 'to the point where it started to feel like my whole life as an adult had been a dream. I almost felt myself disappearing,' she said, 'as though that place could simply take me back into itself. I was sitting by the river one day reading,' she said, 'exactly as I used to do when I was a girl of twelve or thirteen, and everything I had done since then suddenly seemed completely questionable, since it had only brought me back here again to exactly the same spot.'

Returning to the city afterwards she had spent several weeks in a state approaching ecstasy, and had walked over every inch of it, unable to get enough of the familiar feeling of the warm stones beneath her feet.

'Like a married couple on their second honeymoon,' she said. 'Except that unlike my actual marriage, this one has lasted. Also, it's been better for my health.'

Fortunately her ex-husband spent little time in the city, she said, since he raced yachts and was frequently at sea.

'I call him the Buccaneer,' she said. 'When he comes riding into town looking for me, I make sure I am difficult to find.'

She had one child by her husband, a boy of fourteen. They had already separated before the child was born.

'In fact he didn't even know I was pregnant,' she said, 'since I concealed it from him for as long as I could, because I knew I would never have got away from him otherwise. And when he did find out I effectively had to go into hiding, because I am certain he would have tried to kill me. I admit it was selfish of me,' she said, 'to get pregnant in the deliberate way that I did. But I was forty years old and it was really my last chance.'

It had been difficult for her son to gain a perspective on his father, whose long absences and dramatic presences were so unsettling, and whose lifestyle was both brutal and glamorous, while Paola's existence by necessity encompassed all the mundanities of domestic routine. His father had numerous girlfriends, all of them very young and very beautiful, while I, Paola said, am getting old and barely seem like a woman at all any more.

'I am no longer interested in having a man,' she said. 'My body is asking for privacy. It likes hiding under these loose clothes, just as if it was covered with the most disfiguring scars. It has finally cast out my lifelong belief in romantic love,' she said, 'because even at fifty I had somehow kept the idea of finding my true mate, as though he were the hero of a novel who had failed to turn up and had to be tracked down before the novel ended. But my body knows better,' she said, 'and it demands to be left alone.'

We had been walking downhill along a succession of narrow alleys and were now passing through broader, tree-lined streets that occasionally showed glimpses of pleasant squares with fountains and churches along their intersections. This was a very old part of the city, Paola said, which only ten years ago had languished in squalor and neglect, but now money had been spent and it was becoming a popular neighbourhood, with new shops and restaurants opening up and even businesses starting to move here. The shops were the same shops you saw in town centres around the world and the bars and cafés were touristic versions of themselves in the same inevitable way as everywhere else, and so this regeneration,

210

she said, begins to look a little like a mask of death. Europe is dying, she said, and because every separate part is being replaced as it dies it becomes harder and harder to tell what is fake and what is real, so that we might not realise until the whole thing has gone.

She looked at her watch and said that we still had some time before we needed to be at the restaurant; if I didn't mind, there was a place not far away that she thought might interest me. We set off again at an even brisker pace than before, Paola's long fine hair flying out behind her and her silvery tunic flapping and swirling.

'It is a little strange, what we are about to see,' she said as we walked. 'I found it by chance a few years ago. I was passing nearby and the strap of my sandal broke and so I needed somewhere to sit and fix it. I saw that this church was open and I went inside, not thinking anything about it, and I got quite a shock.'

Some fifty years before, she said, the church had been ravaged one night by a terrible fire, whose intensity was such that the very stones had lifted and the leading of the windows melted away, and two of the firefighters had lost their lives putting it out. But instead of restoring the church, the decision was made simply to repair the structural aspects of the building, which continued to be used as a regular place of worship, despite the disturbing extremity of its appearance and the violent events to which that appearance testified.

'Inside it is completely black,' she said, 'and the walls and ceiling are warped like the inside of a cave where the layers of stone have expanded, and the fire, even while it devoured whatever paintings and statues had been there, left everywhere a patina of its own in which one believes one can glimpse ghostly images. Everywhere there are these strange half-shapes like melted wax and then in other places sheared areas where the stonework was split into two by the heat, and empty plinths and alcoves where things are missing, and the texture of the whole thing is so densely affected that it is almost no longer man-made, as if the trauma of the fire had turned it into a natural form. I don't know why,' she said, 'but I find the sight of it extremely moving. The fact that it has been allowed to continue in its true state,' she said, 'when everything else around it has been replaced and cleaned up, has a meaning that I am not quite able to understand or articulate, and yet people continue to go there and act as if everything is normal. At first I thought that someone had made a terrible mistake,' she said, 'in letting it stay like that, as if they thought no one would notice what had happened, and when I saw people inside praying or hearing mass I thought it was indeed possible that some-how they hadn't realised. And this seemed so awful that I wanted to scream at everyone there and force them to look at the black walls and the emptiness. But then I noticed,' she said, 'that in certain places where statues had obviously been, new lights had been installed which illuminated the empty spaces. These lights,' she said, 'had the strange effect of making you see more in the empty space than you would have seen had it been filled with a statue. And so I knew,' she said, 'that this spectacle was not the result of some monstrous neglect or misunderstanding but was the work of an artist.'

We had paused at a traffic light on a busy intersection and were waiting to cross the road. There was no shade, and the air shimmered over the throbbing traffic while the sun pounded unrelentingly on our heads amid the noise. On the other side of the road stood an avenue of great trees like purple clouds in whose grove-like dimness human figures were discernible. People strolled or sat on benches amid the dark trunks and beneath the densely patterned foliage, whose depths of light and shade grew more intricate the more I looked. I saw a woman standing staring absently ahead of her while a small child crouched to examine something at its feet. I saw a man sitting cross-legged on a bench turn the page of his newspaper. A waitress brought a glass to someone sitting at a table and a boy kicked a ball that sped away into the shadows. Birds were pecking imperviously at the ground. The separation between that silent glade-like place and the thundering pavement where we stood seemed for a moment so absolute that it was almost unbearable, as though it represented a disorder so fundamental and insurmountable that any attempt to right it would be ultimately shown to be futile. The lights changed and we began to cross. Sweat was coursing down my back and a pounding had begun in my chest that felt like the extension of the pounding of the sun, as if it had incorporated me into itself.

When we got to the church Paola had described, it was shut. She paced back and forth in front of the locked door as though expecting another way in to present itself.

'It is a shame,' she said. 'I wanted you to see it. I had pictured it,' she said, crestfallen.

The square where we stood was small and well-like and the sun was falling directly into it so that only a rim of shade remained around the edges of the pale shuttered buildings. I leaned against a wall and closed my eyes.

'Are you all right?' I heard Paola say.

After the heat and light of outside, the restaurant was so dark it felt like the middle of the night. A woman was sitting at a table in the furthest corner, beneath a reproduction of Artemisia Gentileschi's *Salome with the Head of Saint John the Baptist*. A bicycle helmet lay on the table in front of her.

'We are very late,' Paola said, and Felícia shrugged, making a grimace with her large mouth that was half-smile and half-frown.

'It's not important,' she said.

We sat down and Paola launched into an explanation of our detour and its failed purpose, while Felícia followed the story patiently with a furrowed brow.

'I don't think I know that place,' she said.

It was just at the bottom of the hill, Paola said, only a few hundred metres away.

'But you arrived by taxi,' Felícia said doubtfully.

That, Paola said, was because of the heat.

'You are hot?' Felícia said to me, apparently surprised. 'It isn't so hot at the moment,' she said. 'At this time of year it can be much worse.'

'But if you aren't used to it,' Paola said, 'it might affect you differently.'

'I suppose it's possible,' Felícia said.

'A little bit goes to the head,' Paola said. 'Like wine. I feel like drinking wine,' she added, reaching for the menu. 'I feel like losing my bearings.'

Felícia nodded slowly.

'It's a good idea,' she said.

She was a tall, spare woman with a long pale face

which in the dim light of the restaurant seemed carved out of deep shadows.

'Let's – what is the expression in English?' Paola said. 'Let's undo our collars.'

'Loosen,' Felícia said. 'Let's loosen our collars.'

'Felícia has a very tight collar,' Paola said, and Felícia gave her strange half-smile half-frown.

'It's not so bad,' she said.

'Very tight,' Paola said, 'but not so much that she chokes. They need to keep you alive, no? You are more useful that way.'

'It's true,' Felícia said, moving her bicycle helmet from the table so that the waiter could put down the wine.

'What's this?' Paola exclaimed. 'Now you are bicycling?'

'I am bicycling,' Felícia said.

'But what happened to your car?' Paola said.

'Stefano took the car away,' Felícia said. She shrugged. 'It belongs to him, after all.'

'But how can you manage without the car?' Paola said. 'You live so far away it's impossible.'

Felícia appeared to think about it.

'It's not impossible,' she said. 'I just have to get up one hour earlier.'

Paola shook her head and swore under her breath.

'What offended me,' Felícia said, 'was his reason

for taking it. He said that he could no longer trust me with the car.'

'Trust you?' Paola said.

'The arrangement has been,' Felícia said slowly, 'that whoever is looking after Alessandra has the car. So if Stefano has her for the weekend, the car goes with her. But most of the time she is with me, so the car stays parked outside my apartment. When something goes wrong with it, Stefano expects me to take care of it. Two weeks ago,' she said, 'it needed entirely new tyres, and it cost almost half my salary for the month to replace them.'

'So it has been to his advantage,' Paola said.

'It was after I replaced the tyres that I received a letter from Stefano's lawyer,' Felícia said. 'The letter said that my salary was not sufficient to justify having a car and to cover the costs of maintaining it. I had not noticed,' she said, 'that the car was gone. I was getting Alessandra ready for school and we were late, but when I read the letter I looked out of the window and saw that the car was not there. Stefano has his own key,' she said, 'so I realised that he must have come during the night and taken it while we were sleeping. I had a very full schedule for that day and it completely depended on having the car, so I was shocked by the fact that he hadn't warned me. But also,' she said, 'I realised that unconsciously I had taken a feeling of security and legitimacy from the car, because even though it was expensive to maintain, the fact that I shared it with Stefano seemed to offer me some kind of protection. Until that moment when I looked out of the window and saw an empty space where the car had been, I had been holding on to a delusion, when even an hour earlier I would have sworn I had no delusions left. And even then,' she said, 'I remained deluded, because I picked up the phone and called Stefano, thinking there must have been some mistake. He was very calm,' she said, 'and he spoke to me as if I was a naughty child that has to have their punishment explained to them, and when I began to cry he became even calmer, and he agreed it was very sad that I brought these misfortunes on myself with my lack of self-control.'

'But that is completely wrong,' Paola exclaimed. 'Your own lawyer can argue that you need the car because you are taking care of the child.'

Felícia nodded slowly.

'I thought so too,' she said. 'And so I called her, even though that kind of conversation is very expensive, and she said there was only one question, which was the question of whose name is on the documents for the car. According to her there was absolutely no moral argument I could make, which I found so impossible to believe that we ended up talking for much too long and so running up an enormous bill on top of everything else. I should have known by now,' she said, 'that Stefano does nothing on the basis of what is right or wrong, but instead acts only according to what the law will allow him to do. He understands that the law can be used as his weapon, where I only think of it in connection with justice, by which time it is far too late.'

'It's unfortunate for you that Stefano is so intelligent,' Paola said, and Felícia smiled.

'It's true that I made sure to choose someone intelligent,' she said.

'The Buccaneer used the law like they use the big ball on the chain to demolish a building,' Paola said. 'It was clumsy and it made a lot of mess, and in the end there was nothing left. Though if it ever becomes legal to kill another person,' she said, 'I will hear a knock on my door before even a minute has passed and it will be him, because although he has been happy to break the law in small ways that won't expose him, he has never liked the idea of serving a prison sentence on my behalf, even for the pleasure of murdering me.'

Felícia sat back in her chair, her wine glass nursed in her lap and her melancholy smile just visible in the shadows.

'The wine is so nice,' she said. 'It makes me feel I could just sleep.'

'You are tired,' Paola said, and Felícia nodded and half-closed her eyes, still smiling.

'This morning,' she said slowly, 'I got up at six, I dropped Alessandra at school at seven and I cycled to the college where I teach translation to give a class at eight. Then I cycled back and caught the train out to the suburbs where I had two English and French classes to teach at the school there. The only problem,' she said, 'was that one of the other teachers was absent today and so there were twice the usual number of students and, since a test had been scheduled, twice the number of papers to take home to mark. I couldn't see how I would be able to carry them on the bicycle. I was quite proud of the solution I came up with,' she said, 'which was to tie the bundle of papers to the seat and cycle home standing up. Then,' she said, 'I took the train into the city and went to the library where I had been asked to give a talk on cataloguing translated texts, before coming here. Alessandra was unwell this morning,' she added, 'and so I had half-expected to get a call from the school saying that I needed to come and collect her, in which case I didn't know what I would have done since my schedule was completely full, but fortunately the call didn't come.

'I did, however, receive another call,' Felícia said, tilting her chair back and resting her head against the wall, 'which was from my mother, saying that she was

220

tired of storing certain boxes and small pieces of furniture that she had agreed to keep for me, and that if
I didn't come and get them by the end of the day she
would be putting them out on the street. I reminded
her,' she said with her strange half-smile half-frown,
'that since I am staying in the apartment of a friend
I have nowhere to put these items, and neither do I
now have a car in which I could come to collect them,
while in her house there is a big attic where they can
sit disturbing nobody. She said she was tired of having
my things in her attic, and repeated that she would
be putting them out on the street if I didn't come and
collect them by the end of the day. It was not her fault,
she said, that I had made such a mess of my life and
that I didn't even have a proper home to live in. You
came from a nice home, she said, and yet you expect
your child to live like a tramp. I said to her, Mama,
it was different for you, because Papa took care of
everything and you didn't have to work. And she said
yes, and look at what all your equality has done for
you – the men no longer respect you and can treat
you like the dirt on their shoe. Your cousin Angela has
never worked, she said, and she has been divorced
two times and is richer than the queen of England,
because she stayed at home and took care of her children and treated them as her asset. But you don't have
a house or any money or even a car, she said, and

your child goes around looking like an orphan on the street. You don't even get her fringe cut, she said, so it covers her eyes and she can't see where she is going. And I said, Mama, Stefano likes her hair that way and he insists that I don't cut it, so there is nothing I can do. And she said, I can't believe I brought such a woman into the world, who allows a man to tell her what to do with her own child's hair. And she repeated that she no longer wanted my possessions in her house and she put down the phone.

'Last night,' Felícia said, 'a friend came to visit us at the apartment, a woman friend Alessandra hadn't met before. We were talking about my work, and Alessandra suddenly interrupted. Mama's always talking about her work, she said to this friend of mine, but in fact it isn't work – what she calls work is what other people would call a hobby. Don't you agree it's a bit of a joke, Alessandra says to this friend, to call it work when all she is doing is sitting reading a book? And the friend says, no, she doesn't agree, and that translation is not only work but also an art. Alessandra looks at her and then she says to me, Mama, who is this person in our apartment? She isn't very well dressed, Alessandra says; in fact she looks like a witch. My friend tried to laugh but I could see she was very upset at being spoken to in this way, especially by a five-year-old child, and I couldn't explain to her in front of Alessandra that this is how Stefano is finally getting his revenge, by poisoning my own child against me and filling her with his own arrogant nature. I remember,' Felícia said, 'when Stefano and I first separated, Stefano took her away with him one day and didn't bring her back. He was meant to have her for only a few hours, and he kept her for ten days and refused to answer my phone calls and messages. During those ten days I nearly went mad with grief: I don't think I slept for more than a few minutes at a time, and I paced around and around our apartment like a trapped animal, waiting for the situation to end. It was only later,' she said, 'that I understood that the pain I endured during those days was not the pain of responsibility. It was not a consequence of my fight with Stefano but rather was the result of calculated cruelty, to the child as well as to myself: his theft of Alessandra was a show of strength and a way of proving his power to me, that he could take her away and bring her back when he chose to. If we had fought physically,' she said, 'he would likewise have won, and this was what he was making clear to me by removing the child at will, that if I thought I had power – even if only the old power of the mother – I was completely mistaken. I had not, moreover, found freedom by leaving him: in fact what I had done was forfeit all my rights, which he had only extended to me in the first place, and made myself his slave. There is a passage in one of your books,' she said to me, 'where you describe enduring something similar, and I translated it very carefully and with great caution, as if it were something fragile that I might mistakenly break or kill, because these experiences do not fully belong to reality and the evidence for them is a matter of one person's word against another's. It was important I didn't get any of the words wrong,' she said, 'and afterwards I felt that while you had legitimised this half-reality by writing about it, I had legitimised it again by managing to transpose it into another language and ensuring its survival.'

'We survive,' Paola said, tilting her empty wine glass to look inside. 'Our bodies outlive their use of them, and that is what annoys them most of all. These bodies continue to exist, getting older and uglier and telling them the truth they don't want to hear. The Buccaneer is still pursuing me even after all these years,' she said, 'making sure that whenever I show a sign of life he is there to crush it. My head is whirling with wine,' she added, with a crooked, mischievous smile, 'just like he used to whirl me around by my hair, except that now it doesn't hurt. That is revenge, no? It used to hurt so much when he pulled my hair,' she said, 'so it is good to talk about these things when your head is whirling with wine instead, and with the picture of the man's severed head on a plate before my eyes. What I don't understand,' she said to me, 'is why you have married again, when you know what you know. You have put it in writing,' she said, 'and that brings with it all the laws.'

I hoped to get the better of those laws, I said, by living within them. My older son had once made a copy of that painting on the wall, I said, except that he had left out all the detail and merely blocked in the forms and the spatial relationships between them. What was interesting, I said, was that without those details and the story to which they were associated, the painting became a study not of murderousness but of the complexity of love.

Paola slowly shook her head.

'It isn't possible,' she said. 'Those laws are for men and maybe for children. But for women it's just an illusion, like the sandcastle on the beach, which after all is only how the child proves his nature, by building the temporary edifice until he too can become a man. In law the woman is temporary, between the permanence of the land and the violence of the sea. It is better to be invisible,' she said. 'It is better to live outside the law. To be a – what is the word in English?'

'An outlaw,' Felícia said, grinning in the shadows.

'An outlaw,' Paola said, satisfied. She raised her

empty glass and clinked it against Felícia's. 'I choose to live as an outlaw.'

The taxi driver had pointed the way to the beach from the place on the road where he dropped me, making sweeping gestures with his arms to convey the necessity for continuing to walk out beyond the boardwalk, which curved away among the dunes out of sight. The blank, heavy heat of the afternoon had begun to break down and a soft bruised colour had come into the sky. The white cement of the low wall bordering the sand held the residue of the day's glare against a sharp line of encroaching shadow. The muffled sound of the water rose from beyond the dunes, and there was suddenly the sea's feeling of weight and extension, despite the fact that it was out of sight.

My phone rang and the screen showed my younger son's name.

'There's been a bit of a disaster,' he said.

Tell me, I said.

It happened late last night, he said. He and some friends had accidentally started a fire, he said. There had been some damage and he was worried about what the consequences would be.

There was no point phoning you because you were away, he said. But then I couldn't get hold of Dad either.

I asked him whether he was all right. I asked him how on earth it had happened, and what he had been thinking of.

'Faye,' he said fractiously, 'will you just listen?'

He and another boy and a girl were at a friend's flat for the evening. The flat was in a block that had a gym and a swimming pool in the basement. At around midnight the three of them had decided to go swimming, and had gone with their towels and their swimming costumes downstairs. They had used the changing rooms, but when the boys had left the men's changing room the door had swung shut and locked behind them. The other boy had left his towel in there, draped over a heater. Within a few minutes, they saw through the changing room window that the towel had caught fire. There was a pool cleaner with a long handle leaning against a wall, my son said, and so I grabbed it and I broke the window and I managed to hook up the towel and pull it back through the window and we put it out. There was broken glass everywhere, he said, and the whole pool house was full of smoke and then an alarm went off and all these people started to come running in. They were shouting at us and accusing us of vandalising the building and we kept trying to explain what had happened but they wouldn't listen to us. The other two had stepped in the glass, he said, and their feet were bleeding and they were crying because they were so frightened, but these people just kept shouting in our faces. One of them was talking about his children, he said, who were asleep in the flat on the floor above, and he kept saying how traumatised they would have been to wake up and find there was smoke in their bedroom, even though they hadn't actually woken up. They took our names and addresses and said they were going to call the police, he said, and then they went away. We stayed there and I cleared up all the glass and I spent hours picking the pieces out of the other two's feet. They were both really upset, he said, and after a while I told them to just go home, and that I would wait there for the police to come. And I waited and waited, he said, but the police didn't come. I waited all night, he said, and in the end I just left and went to school.

He began to cry.

All day I've been expecting someone to come and call me out of class, he said. I don't know what to do.

I asked him whether it was permitted to swim in the pool at night.

Yes, he wailed. People do it all the time. And it wasn't our fault about the door, because my friend told me it was broken and that they were meant to be fixing it. I know we were stupid to put the towel on the heater but there wasn't a sign telling you not to and we didn't realise it could catch fire. I don't know why the police didn't come, he said. I almost wish they had, because I don't know what to do now.

They didn't come, I said, because you didn't do anything wrong.

He was silent.

In fact, I said, you ought to be congratulated, because it was a good idea to use the pool cleaner and the building might have caught fire otherwise.

I've written a letter, he said presently. I did it during break. It explains everything that happened. I thought I would take it there and leave it for people to read.

There was a silence.

When are you coming home? he said.

Tomorrow, I said.

Can I come over? he said, and then he said: Sometimes I feel as if I'm about to fall over the edge of something, and that there'll be nothing and no one to catch me.

You're tired, I said. You've been awake all night.

I feel so lonely, he said, and yet I have no privacy. People just act as if I'm not there. I could be doing anything, he said. I could be slitting my wrists and they would neither know nor care.

It isn't your fault, I said.

They ask me things, he said, but they don't connect the things up. They don't relate them to things I've

229

already told them. There are just all these meaningless facts.

You can't tell your story to everybody, I said. Maybe you can only tell it to one person.

Maybe, he said.

Come when you feel like it, I said. I can't wait to see you.

The sky had turned a dull red and a breeze had picked up that made the dry grasses amid the dunes sway back and forth. The boardwalk was deserted and I followed it until I came out on to a stretch of beach. It was wild and strewn with litter and the sea was roiling and crashing where the beach shelved downwards to the water. The wind was stronger here and the dunes were sending their lengthening, mountainous shadows across the rough greyish sand. Amid the shadows I saw human figures, crouching or standing or sitting. They were arranged mostly in pairs and they were either still or moved around intimately and absorbedly as if bent on some primitive task. A short distance away there was a fire made of driftwood and the wind sent the smoke whirling upwards. There were more figures gathered around the fire and the lit ends of their cigarettes made piercing orange points in the dusky light. I could sometimes hear the low sounds of conversation, which the wind and the sea's crashing then blotted out.

I began to walk amid the figures up the beach. They were men, either naked or sometimes wearing a simple loincloth. Some of them were hardly more than boys. They were mostly silent as I passed, and either looked away or seemed not to see me, though one or two stared at me frankly and expressionlessly. A boy of startling beauty glanced into my eyes and glanced away again, burying his face shyly into the thick muscled shoulder of his companion. He was kneeling and I saw the rounded shapes of his buttocks beneath the other man's large hand. I walked on, past the group who were gathered round the fire and who turned to look at me like animals surprised in a grove. The strange red light had spread across the sky in a great stain tinged with yellow and black. Far in the distance the buildings of the dock and the suburbs stood dimly in a smudgy haze of surf. I found an empty stretch of sand and I began to take off my clothes. A few feet away the sea heaved and churned, brimful and restless, streaked with red and grey. The wind was stronger beyond the dunes and a fine rain of sand blew against my skin. I went down to the water, pressing quickly forward through the barging waves. The beach shelved so steeply that I was quickly sucked out into the moving mass, whose density and power seemed to keep me effortlessly on the surface so that I rose and fell along with its undulations. The men had turned to watch me. One of them got to his feet, a huge burly man with a great curling black beard and a rounded stomach and thighs like hams. Slowly he walked down towards the water's edge, his white teeth faintly glimmering through his beard in a smile, his eyes fixed on mine. I looked back at him from my suspended distance, rising and falling. He came to a halt just where the waves broke and he stood there in his nakedness like a deity, resplendent and grinning. Then he grasped his thick penis and began to urinate into the water. The flow came out so abundantly that it made a fat, glittering jet, like a rope of gold he was casting into the sea. He looked at me with black eyes full of malevolent delight while the golden jet poured unceasingly forth from him until it seemed impossible that he could contain any more. The water bore me up, heaving, as if I lay on the breast of some sighing creature while the man emptied himself into its depths. I looked into his cruel, merry eyes, and I waited for him to stop.